6 thrilling tales

VACATION'S END

STANDARD ISSUE SPIRITS

WHERE DID THEY COME FROM?

SURvIVe

CUT-UP

A FATAL THING

W.G. TUTTLE

6 thrilling tales

VACATION'S END

STANDARD ISSUE SPIRITS

WHERE DID THEY COME FROM?

SURVIVE

CUT-UP

A FATAL THING

A Collection of Short Stories

THIS IS A
W.G. TUTTLE
BLURRED INK, LLC
BOOK PRODUCTION

Riveting fiction.

Novels
Those Who Long
Try To Sleep
October Midnight
War For The Spheres

Short Stories
Adamah - A Book of the Serpent
Scranton October 1894
SURvIVe
Cut-Up
Where Did THEY Come From?
Standard Issue Spirits
Vacation's End
A Fatal Thing

1-Where Did THEY Come From?
Published as standalone short story. ISBN: 978-1-949637-09-0
Copyright © 2019 by W. G. TUTTLE, i.e. Walter George Tuttle, Jr.

2-Standard Issue Spirits
Published as standalone short story. ISBN: 978-1-949637-08-3
Copyright © 2019 by W. G. TUTTLE, i.e. Walter George Tuttle, Jr.

3-Vacation's End
Published as standalone short story. ISBN: 978-1-949637-07-6
Copyright © 2019 by W. G. TUTTLE, i.e. Walter George Tuttle, Jr.

4-A Fatal Thing
Published as standalone short story. ISBN: 978-1-949637-06-9
Copyright © 2019 by W. G. TUTTLE, i.e. Walter George Tuttle, Jr.

5- CUT-UP
Published as standalone short story. ISBN: 978-1-949637-20-5
Copyright © 2020 by W. G. TUTTLE, i.e. Walter George Tuttle, Jr.

6- SURVIVE
Published as standalone short story. ISBN: 978-1-949637-21-2
Copyright © 2020 by W. G. TUTTLE, i.e. Walter George Tuttle, Jr.

For my wife Shawn

6 thrilling short stories that will assault your imagination.

In **Vacation's End**, the Keifers are a typical American family. What would cause them to cut all ties with the world and leave for a vacation?

In **Standard Issue Spirits**, everyone has a spirit, but is each one unique? Raimonds decides he is going to find the answer. How he goes about it will shock you.

In **Where Did THEY Come From?**, the horror stories Sorrel writes are presumably from his mind's eye. But are they imagined or real?

In **SURVIVE**, an invisible, odorless predator preys on living tissue, growing more powerful by the second, replicating and spreading on every continent of the globe. Under mandatory quarantine conditions, Ray ventures into the city for something his wife needs. Will he SURVIVE? Will the world SURVIVE?

In **CUT-UP**, it is Halloween. Rennis' mask is his sliced-up face. That is not all he cuts up. Has he gone mad? Or is there an insidious evil lurking to seduce him?

In **A Fatal Thing**, otherworldly beings invade Earth. Dr. Gombya takes matters into his own hands to save the world.

Stories Included

Where Did THEY Come From?	1
Standard Issue Spirits	29
Vacation's End	69
A Fatal Thing	107
CUT-UP	120
SURvIVE	168

Where Did

They

Come From?

1

Everyone should pay attention to what their mind's eye shows them. Call those images whatever you like: dreams, daymares, nightmares, visions, hallucinations, sleep, or a trance—it doesn't matter. Languages are full of synonyms, meaning the same thing, yet, mean nothing.

No one is more susceptible to the mind's eye suggestion than the fiction writer. Electronic screens, paper, and anything writers can get their hands on becomes the Ouija Board and the keyboard, writing utensil, or any item used to record what they see is the planchette.

Nonwriters think writers sit down and plan what they are going to write. And, unfortunately, they would be correct with some writers outlining their stories, complete with character profiles and avatars. It works for some, but not most, but who's to judge.

There's another type of writer: one who doesn't try to conjure stories. For the stories, themselves, compete for airtime in the mind's eye. Compete doesn't mean running a race. Instead, think of gladiators fighting to survive. It's brutal. Just beyond the lens of that mysterious portal called the mind's eye is perhaps the bloodiest battlefield that exists, yet doesn't.

Sure, a few regrettable stories make it out and are published for the world to see, but, overall, only the strongest stories survive. Often, the strongest means the nastiest. Of course, this doesn't mean the story should be immediately classified as horror. For horror can be found in any genre.

Writers already dabbling in the forbidden may decide to take it further. Images in the mind's eye are carried out in real life to ensure the senses are indeed present and experienced in the imagination. Not acted out as in a fictional performance. They are carried out as in executed for real with equally real consequences. Entering the territory beyond the forbidden goes beyond writing—beyond storytelling—beyond inspiration.

Or does it? Isn't the writer charged with writing the story that has fought so hard to live no matter the content?

Sorrel thought so.

2

Out of breath, Sorrel rolled off the woman on his bed and onto his back. Sweat glistened pale skin on his slender body. Catching his breath, he rolled out of bed—the woman laying there not worth a second glance.

It wasn't because she wasn't beautiful, she was, by anyone's standard. Sorrel had a gentleman's appearance and carried himself as such, which served him well in attracting women. Eccentricities in his mannerisms projected an arrogance that most women perceived as confidence.

Devotion to his work and himself summed up his life. A low point had stripped him of nearly everything and Sorrel escaped his troubles in his work—writing horror stories. All of the frustration, disappointment, and fear poured out of him through his mind's eye onto paper.

Negative experiences in life had darkened the lens—blackened as if coated by hell's infernal ashes. Every imagination on the other side, no matter how wholesome or foul, filtered through to the physical world smoldering and warped worse than how they began.

Expression born out of Sorrel's frustration, disappointment, anger, and jealousy found life in the pixels of his computer, resembling ink, creating shapes of letters into words, sentences, and paragraphs into stories. A writer, he recorded them, without applying any filtering responsibility of his own. And his fans awarded him, buying his work and living vicariously through the characters in his stories.

Who didn't want a successful revenge? A carefree sex-life? To be the lowest of the low inexplicably elevated to the highest of highs and get away with anything—including murder?

Sorrel's readers absorbed his stories as possibilities in their own lives through blackened lenses of their own mind's eye. The religious, the scum of the Earth— sometimes the same thing—and others relished a life far removed from their own.

The human condition spanned every condition of man, yet, common conditions were found in every man for they are human and distinct enough not to equalize life for everyone. And those conditions, common and uncommon, impacted Sorrel's life and work.

Work was his life and his life was spent on work. There was no separating the two. For his work as a writer found potential permanency in published stories. The desires of his heart materialized into all he had longed for.

As stories traversed through Sorrel's lens of his mind's eye with ease, his physical eyes became blind, unable to accurately measure the degrees because the lines at each degree had become so twisted, they intertwined, not realizing that his writing had entered the taboo, instead thinking he merely wrote in the gray and his readers could decide for themselves whether or not he had crossed the line.

With the lines twisted and intertwined, crossed he had— beyond the forbidden; premeditated as if buying a one-way plane ticket to take him there.

A single bang on the front door of his high-rise apartment startled Sorrel; the just-swallowed brandy nearly choking him. Perhaps his plane ticket had arrived.

3

Naked and leaning against a sliding glass door, Sorrel stared at the front door. No other knock came—as agreed on how it would go. Despite the interrupted swallow a moment ago, he gulped the rest of the brandy in his sifter and worked it harshly down his throat to get it in him. Setting the glass on the desk, he walked toward the door.

By the time he had arrived, blood had filled and hardened his penis in an erection. An index finger swiveled the hinge on the door guard and he reached for the handle, then retracted as if unsure.

The patience of the knocker on the other side amazed Sorrel. If it were him out there, nervous anxiety would have him banging on the door to get inside and out of the hallway before being seen. Whoever was out there was a professional in such matters. Sorrel was not. A big difference.

Sorrel turned the doorknob, opened it an inch, and backed away from the door, unsure.

The door remained like that and he wondered if the knocker wasn't as patient as he had thought and left before being seen.

Then, the door swung open a little farther.

A tentacle of black smoke streamed into the apartment as if peeking.

Afraid, Sorrel stepped back.

More smoke tentacles became visible out from behind the door and then a black mass appeared with streamers of black smoke emitting from it. How, Sorrel didn't know and didn't want to know, retreating to his writing desk.

The smokey mass floated into the apartment, slowly as if as unsure as Sorrel, bringing with it a peculiarly dressed body.

Leaving the door open, the otherworldly slithered toward Sorrel on whatever moved it under its cloak dragging on the floor. Its entire appearance flickered like a channel losing reception on an old television. Then, it disappeared.

Afraid to move, even breathe, Sorrel waited.

Impatience raised his hand. That's as far as it got. Fear held it back. The whole idea of feeling in front of him, feeling for the thing, for some kind of resolution stemmed out of necessity rather than bravery—so he could breathe again.

It reappeared—closer this time, closer than Sorrel would have expected.

Fear stiffened Sorrel's body, a standing corpse, and paused his breathing longer.

Domineering, the figure only hell could devise loomed threateningly near, then, its form flickered into oblivion as it had done before.

Sorrel's fear-frozen body fought against itself to move because Sorrel mistook the flicker for movement and tried to protect himself. This contradiction messed up his body.

Which only worsened when the writer awkwardly sidestepped to get around the desk and the sinister creep materialized again, mere inches away from Sorrel's bare body.

Sorrel's body cowered smaller as did his erection but his wide eyes remained fixated on this ... what? He didn't know.

Strangely, no temperature of any kind transferred from it onto Sorrel's nude body. Nor did it emit an odor. This could be a dream. Had to be. A terrible mistaken nightmare delivered by a mare to the wrong person.

Entertaining the notion, Sorrel reached for the desk behind him, picked up the sifter, and cracked himself on top of the head with it. The stem broke and the bowl fell to the rug.

His head hurt. Bad. Too much force had been applied to the blow, leaving no room for error as to whether this was a dream or real. The bottom stem, still in his fingers, was set on the desk as if the bowl were still on it.

It was real. All of it. Including its strange cloak, which looked like it was made out of paper—typing paper or computer paper. What difference did it make? White paper with typing on it.

Looking closer, Sorrel made out some words: **dead, kill, murder**—he'd seen enough. Frantically, he slid around the desk to the sliding glass doors. On his way, his bare foot pressed down on the glass bowl of the sifter and broke it, but was too frightened to notice. With his hand gripping the handle of the sliding door, all he could think about now were life-ending thoughts. Where they came from, he wasn't sure.

4

The blackness slithered and flickered toward Sorrel. Sorrel opened the sliding glass door and the wind entered the apartment.

For a time, it was as if the wind had blown away the apparition because Sorrel no longer saw it.

Shockingly and threateningly the visitor reappeared before Sorrel, only closer this time—just enough space between them, so they didn't touch. Everything stilled: time, motion, the wind. Black smoke slow-motioned around its head; particles floated within the smoke. Something moved slowly and deliberately behind the fog. Movement from something faster sped across the head, smearing the smoke like a plane flying through a cloud, then disappeared.

Fear chipped away some of Sorrel's manhood while the cool wind shriveled his physical manhood close to his body. Standing naked and trapped between this thing and the screen that led to a tiny balcony on the twenty-seventh floor, he hated being exposed. Whatever moved under the smoke made matters worse. At any time something could emerge from it.

During an attempt by Sorrel to slide out from between this horror story and the screen, the wind returned in full-force, blowing the smoke back off the visitor's head like windblown hair, exposing underneath.

It was awful. A bat consumed some moths Sorrel had mistaken as floating particles. A raven snapped its beak at a scurrying rodent. A snake, coiled around the head, widened its mouth around the bat and another snakehead appeared, parted its mouth, and went for the raven.

Blood from Sorrel's cut foot stained the carpet, tracking his regression, as he fell through the screen onto the concrete slab of the balcony.

The monstrosity followed and looked down at Sorrel. A confused night with windblown smears of purple and bluish-gray captured the horror. The wind whipped around them, raising goosebumps all over the writer's pale skin higher, and keeping the brutal side of nature around the thing's head exposed.

Strangely, as one snake consumed a bat consuming moths and another snake swallowed a raven attacking a rodent, the process continually repeated without ever changing the size of the head.

Sounds of movement and consumption repeatedly relived expounded their gruesomeness over the blustering wind. Other than predator eating prey, all other known laws of life no longer made sense out here on the balcony. Whatever force had maintained order in the world had left, accentuating the experience.

Moth wings sounded like helicopter blades cutting through the air. Bat chirps squeaked excitedly like a honing device zeroing in on what it searched for and then the collapse of the moth's carcass. A snake's snatch of a bat, then the breaking. A guttural croak of a raven on the attack; its beak clamping on the rodent; scratchy squeaks followed and then the tearing of hair, skin, and flesh. Another snake's catch of the raven and constrictive crushing.

This was Sorrel's doing. If he experienced a similar fate tonight—a breaking—there was no one else to blame. Earlier in the evening, before taking the woman to dinner and bringing her back to the apartment for some drinks and more, he had logged into his computer, entered the black web, and hired what he had thought to be a person to come to the apartment to do a deed he could never do himself.

The hiring hadn't been done on a whim. No Sorrel had carefully researched for who he had thought might be the right individual for the job. Not this damned thing standing over him. It must think Sorrel was who the request had been made for.

Realizing this, Sorrel pointed toward the inside of the apartment. Maybe order could be found inside, but he doubted it.

While holding his hand there, his eyes wandered, reading more words and phrases typed on the paper cloak. **Baby killer**. An infant's cry sounded on the balcony when he read it, then it ceased. **Spontaneous human combustion**. A burst of flame whined as if ignited in the unsettled wind outside followed by panicked wails of an adult male, surprised—and burning—that faded away. **Hacked to pieces**. Grotesque forceful entries of something wedged being whacked into an unwilling target followed by squishy suctions upon withdrawal were sounds a writer didn't need to see to understand. These sounds, too, faded into the wind.

Eyeless other than the ones on the living things consuming each other around its head, the hired-hand seemed to look down at Sorrel; a never-ending cycle of snake-bat-moth and snake-raven-rodent repeated around its head over-and-over again.

Finally, the written word of abomination backed away. Sorrel took it as a good sign and possibly understanding, making sure to keep pointing to inside the apartment.

As the thing moved, a banging sound intensified above all others. At first, Sorrel thought it was the frame of the screen because of the wind. When he checked, the frame vibrated within its tracks, but that wasn't what he heard. This sound reminded him more of ... well ... typing.

Wanting out of the confused night that had probably seeped into his brain, making him confused, Sorrel stood. Athletically, his body curved as he moved around the threat as if dodging a tag in the childhood game.

This wasn't a game. Not now. Foolish for him to think it ever was. Maybe it had started that way, but this had escalated into something he wished he had never done.

But what was done was done. Why waste this now when he had probably endured the worst?

So, Sorrel didn't waste it. More confident now, he walked naked toward the bedroom and accusingly pointed inside.

The woman on the bed saw the crazed look on Sorrel's face and the walking hell coming up behind and tried to get up, but the straps around her wrists and ankles held her there. Repeated attempts at screams failed as the gag in her mouth reduced them to moans.

Her face turned red from the strain and veins surfaced in her neck, while she arched her back for leverage to break free —which also failed.

5

Staring at the auburn-haired beauty, the infernal glided toward her on whatever was underneath its manuscript of horrible words and phrases.

All of the amplified sounds Sorrel had heard outside were no more. Perhaps a remnant of order still lingered inside the apartment.

As Sorrel watched hell itself close-in on the captive woman, it occurred to him *it* was happening. With some order restored, his tired arm dropped to his side and he trotted, nude, to his desk, leaving blood stains on the carpet from his wounded foot.

As he sat down, the hard-on had returned, so he adjusted himself comfortably.

In moving the mouse, the manuscript he had been working on appeared on the computer screen—another horror story about unexplainable deaths occurring all over Paris, France.

He put on his writing glasses and didn't waste any time punching the keys, recording what he saw. There was no questioning it: his fingers typing away on the keys matched the banging sound he had heard earlier. And what he saw was money in the bank and awards. Terrible things he had imagined had made it into his stories, but the hellion before him would never have been conceived. So, he typed frantically, afraid of missing anything.

There'll be some critics who will say he crossed the line. To hell with them. Who has the power to define what is forbidden? A person? An organization? A group? Such an idea went beyond dumb. Censorship in just about every media medium continued to lessen anyway, so why not leap ahead into the future and get rid of restrictions altogether.

Other critics will read his expression of uncensored art and love it. Praises will outway the public outcry, but both will fuel the novel's success. Publicity, whether good or bad, especially in today's twenty-four-seven news coverage, would catapult him to the top of the rankings—and, hopefully, earnings. Those who approve won't be able to wait to read it. Some of the opposition will read it just to see what the fuss is all about. Sales were sales and no writer ever complained about nor cared who was buying or why.

Besides, no one will ever know about what was happening in the apartment or that it was real. Readers who read the story will *believe* it and *see* it in their mind's eye if he captured it in his writing, but will go on thinking at worst that he has a sick imagination. No writer would have the balls to stage a murder to capture it on the page.

The creature stood beside the bed, looking down at the hysterical woman. Facing Sorrel's view, the scene was perfect.

A throbbing erection made the whole damn thing perfect and Sorrel punched the keys faster.

An appendage appeared out from the paper cloak.

Sorrel squinted, trying to make it out. Its form wasn't a five-fingered human hand. Instead, it resembled a nubbed wrist with the hand cut off.

The appendage thrust forward like a dagger into her crotch.

Sorrel's ached from the pressure; he was so hard.

When the appendage pulled back out, flesh and bodily

fluids graffitied the air.

The writer stared. Catching himself not working, he returned to typing.

The moths left the beast's head and entered the woman there, followed by the rodent, the bat, the raven, a snake, and the other snake.

"Oh, God!" Sorrel said to himself because of what he saw and the ache in his privates. Redfaced and nearly in tears, he watched the abomination and typed frantically in his hysteria, recording everything, including his own pain and torment that he reflected onto the victim in his story and his turned-on rage inside the murderer.

After concentrating on the entry point and the movement going on under the women's skin, Sorrel finally looked up at hell's Bible.

Out of the black atmosphere, hovering around its head, a single human eye peeked through, staring out of the bedroom and into the other room at the writer.

6

Pee warmed Sorrel's thighs and buttocks as it gathered on the leather chair. The God-like feeling Sorrel had felt vanished. He felt more exposed now than he had when the killer stood within an inch of him by the balcony glass doors. Every ounce of the adrenalized high he had felt only a moment ago had drained out of him in his pee.

The woman laid still on the bed. Other than her stomach raising and lowering, not from breathing, but from the living things inside her. When they exited, they all seemed a little bigger—even the moths.

Nude and sitting in his own urine, Sorrel wept as he typed. Emotion poured out of him into the manuscript. Thoughts of sales, awards, and who would love it or not no longer occupied the writer's mind. He was writing—genuinely writing—as a writer should, seeing the story unfold in front of him and recording what he saw.

Clickety-clack of the keyboard keys and the occasional whine from Sorrel were the only sounds in the apartment.

The manuscript of terror with its smoking head floated out of the bedroom, while the woman lay on the bed behind—dead.

That'll be the cover, Sorrel thought, not looking at the

computer screen, instead watching the killer advance toward him and typing what he saw.

The thing stopped in front of the desk and waited.

"Almost done," Sorrel said, typing away.

The typing slowed; the magic was ending.

Finished with what he wanted to get down, Sorrel asked, "Where would you like the payment made?"

The question seemed stupid, now. It had been his expectation a human would have come. Not an unexplainable supernatural. What would such a thing need with money?

A coin sat on the desk. Not a metallic one, but ivory—perhaps made of bone.

Staring at it, Sorrel never saw it placed there.

Looking up at the blackness, Sorrel simply said, "Alright. I'll contact the cleanup guy."

With that, the evil glided toward the sliding glass doors instead of the front door in which it had come and disappeared through them.

The writer didn't move from the chair. Sensing it was gone, the deed now over, he burst into tears; the anguish made it hard to breathe.

7

The darkness inside Sorrel had turned a few shades darker. It had always been there; it's how he had written those horror stories loved by millions. Referring to it as *the* darkness was accurate because no one ever said it all belonged to Sorrel.

There had been plenty of times while writing *the* darkness inside had scared the hell out of him. And if hell had been scared out of him, then what darkness remained?

All he knew was how he felt in the apartment alone. Paranoid and feeling watched when no one else was around. Or was there—looking inside-out—of Sorrel?

Spooking himself had always been the magic. If he was frightened writing the story, how could the reader not be? Just once, he wished he knew nothing about the formulation of the written work and read it like a customer who had no idea what's coming.

Sorrel's active imagination made him swear he had seen the dead woman move in the bedroom. A single knock on the front door made him shiver. All that time had passed and he never put on any clothes.

Sorrel opened the door a crack as he had done before and waited, expecting the cleanup guy he had hired from the black web to dispose of the mess the last visitor had made. Again the door remained cracked open for a time and no one entered.

Not wanting to, he peeked around the door and no one was there. A clipped stack of paper sat on the hallway floor in front of the door, similar to a delivered newspaper.

Right away he knew it wasn't a newspaper. Probably a manuscript someone had left for him to read, thinking he would actually do something with it on their behalf. Naked, he stepped into the hall, looked around, picked up the manuscript, carried it into the apartment, closed the door, and locked it.

Setting the work down on his desk, he noticed the name typed on the manuscript, then the title. It was his—a story about a demon-possessed girl—a bestseller.

Frantically, he went to his manuscript pile to check if it was one of his originals. There wasn't a copy in his pile. The one on the desk must have been taken from it, but how? By whom?

Flipping through the pages and stopping to read a section, he still spotted errors and things he would like to fix even after editors and many others had seen the script numerous times before going to publication.

The pages started flipping on their own and Sorrel backed his hand away. Letters detached from the fibers of the pages and flew into the air like squadrons of planes ordered into battle.

As they floated into the air about a foot or two above the manuscript, the black ink of printed letters transformed into flies—something he remembered writing into that particular story.

Hoards of them from each page swarmed toward the bedroom. Once there, they landed on the dead woman's body, completely covering her.

The flies clung to her for some time, until her form began to shrink and eventually flatten until there was nothing left of her on the bed. Even the straps that had held her down and the gag rag had been consumed.

The cleanup person had arrived—just not as a person.

Witnessing this, Sorrel ran into the bedroom, picked up her high heels, and tossed them onto the bed. When they were devoured by the flies, he threw her clothes and purse on the bed to be destroyed, too. Looking around, he didn't see anything else that had belonged to her.

The car, he thought. Then he remembered he had picked her up.

A buzzing sound came from his cell phone, so he checked it as he wandered into the main room. It was an alarm, notifying him that his car had been broken into.

He thought twice about calling the cops, but with all of the evidence gone, why not. It was the first thing he had purchased when he had come into a good bit of money from his writing.

In front of the sliding glass doors, he dialed the police and waited for an answer. Casually turning around, something large startled him and he dropped the phone. It landed in such a way that the call ended.

Before him stood something just as bizarre as the last visitor. Instead of black smoke circling the head, black flies swarmed it and its paper cloak consisted of blank white pages without text—for they were the flies circling its head.

At the part of the head that faced Sorrel, flies began to avoid an area there and a tunneled hole formed. As it receded all the way, revealing human skin, an eye opened, human, similar to the last in the smoke.

Sorrel blacked out and fell to the rug.

When he awoke a day later, there was another ivory coin lying on the desk.

8

Months had passed and Sorrel's newly published horror novel had been met with both fanfare and opposition just as he had expected. This and his stolen car had deflected the case of the missing woman off him.

No sweat. Sorrel had already purchased a new car, a fully-loaded sports car, more expensive than the last in anticipation of booming sales from the new book. And as far as companionship, they were already lining up to snag the catch of the year.

Still, those damned visitors haunted him. Sleep was still hard to come by, especially the hours after first laying down. Usually, it wasn't until the last hours of the morning he fell asleep before the alarm clock went off. Unless he had an appearance, most mornings he hit the snooze to steal an hour or two.

Images of the woman and what had happened to her haunted him more than the death of the woman itself.

The darkness within Sorrel had turned quite a few shades darker that night. And the darkness stayed. It impacted his outlook on life, relationships, even what he said in the media. One article in particular written about him wondered if he was just cocky, or didn't give a shit anymore.

Both were probably true. Sales and success had made him very confident in his abilities, while not caring about what the media said about him.

He cared more about why the payments he had made per the instructions on the ivory coins to the black web visitors had been returned. The transactions clearly showed the money leaving the account, then being deposited right back in.

9

The first night in his new home came with much anticipation. Getting out of the apartment seemed like the end-all cure. The end of bad visions. Bad dreams. And not sleeping.

Oh, he still held onto the apartment, just in case the magic of writing at the new place wasn't transporting him into the story as had happened at the apartment.

Calling the new place *home* was an understatement. It was *his* home, of course, but the mansion was stately and nothing like the apartment nor anything he had ever lived in before. Many earned a living sufficient enough to live in a similar apartment, but only a select few could afford what he would call from now on *the estate*.

Pleased with himself and his new surroundings, he got into a large, four-post bed, turned off the light, and closed his eyes. Contentment had kept him awake, thinking about how his life had changed from humble beginnings to a gradual buildup to this and that same contentment eventually put him to sleep.

The change was good. Very good.

Bells rang throughout the house, waking Sorrel. Not used to

them, he didn't know what they were until he remembered they were the doorbell—an old French-styled design where the caller pulled on a handle outside and the wires ran to the bells, ringing them.

He had also forgotten that the help wouldn't be arriving until tomorrow. The bells only rang once, so he thought perhaps it had been the wind and fell back to sleep.

Swatting at something pestering his face, Sorrel sat up in bed, irritated. An opened-mouthed something lashed out at his face and he backed away, hitting the back of his head on the headboard.

A hissing snake bobbed and weaved in mid-air. Moths flew just above the covers. Behind them and the snake was the black smoke head and manuscript cloak of the murderer, standing at the foot of the bed.

Behind it was the moth-headed cleaner, standing next to the writing desk from the apartment with the computer on it.

How the two hellions had found him, he didn't know. Or why. Or how the desk and computer were in the bedroom, for he had left the desk back at the apartment and the computer in the downstairs den.

The dancing snake struck at his face again, followed by the second snake in a one-two punch attack. The second's reach was longer than the first and the back of Sorrel's head hit the headboard harder than the first time.

The unwanted visitor by the bed pointed to the desk and computer in the same way Sorrel had pointed to the woman in the bedroom back at the apartment.

Sorrel swatted moths as he got out of bed and the snakes once more reached their fangs out for him in hissing anger, nearly striking the back of his offending hand. He stopped swatting at the moths and sat down at his desk.

On the screen was the first dark website where he had hired the killer. Sorrel's cell phone on the desk in front of him was making an outbound call. It wasn't there before.

But neither were the visitors, desk, or computer.

Sorrel picked up the cell phone and waited. A call-waiting beep let him know another call was coming in. The first call was placed on hold and he answered the second.

"Hello."

Screwy phones. For his own voice sounded back at him.

"Yes, hello. Sorrel here."

Again, he heard his own voice.

While he looked down at the phone in disgust, the phone number jumped out at him. So did the one on the dark website. They were the same.

Returning to the outgoing call, he noticed that number was the same as the incoming number and the number on the website. And that phone number belonged to him.

When he raised his eyes in disbelief, the website on the computer screen had changed to the cleaner's. That contact number, too, was Sorrel's cell number.

But what did it mean?

10

Both visitors stood before the desk. Their cloaks began to come undone, unwrinkling and flattening into individual pages, which combined into one stack of paper on the desk. Moths, rodents, the bat and raven, and the two snakes left the smokey head and entered into the pages where, upon touching them, that part of them disappeared until they were gone entirely as if entering a time portal.

Sorrel thought of the woman on the bed and how they had entered her.

As the bottom of the cloak came undone, what had moved the killer and cleaner around in that spectral gliding fashion became apparent. A writer, Sorrel knew exactly what they were—letters, which stamped onto the organizing pages in the form of words, sentences, paragraphs, and chapters of masterful communication.

It made sense to him now that the words carried the day in storytelling as it had carried the monsters.

Simultaneously, the black smoke began to dissipate off the killer's head as did the last remaining moths from the cleaner's head. A pinkish-purple of something hid underneath each. The more the smoke and moths cleared, the more Sorrel could see.

More pink now, Sorrel swore it reminded him of flesh. Like flesh under fur on a dog's belly.

What resembled human chins appeared first. Then human mouths. More blackness left, revealing human noses. Human eyes peeked out of dark veils until they, too, had become fully exposed. Lastly, human hair. But by then, Sorrel had already recognized the unveiled heads.

"Yes, hello. Sorrel here," sounded out of the cell phone on the desk in Sorrel's voice.

It repeated, *"Sorrel here," "Sorrel here," "Sorrel here…"*

Indeed, Sorrel was here. For the heads on the killer and the cleaner were Sorrel's.

For the moths had eaten away all of the light inside him, leaving a smoldering darkness ever-building until it could no longer be contained and needed to be carried out. Imagination was no longer sufficient.

A single page, floating like a magic carpet, landed on top of the stack of paper—the title page, the last page the first, completing the manuscript. It wasn't a title he recognized working on, but the *by* name was clearly his.

Lovingly, the dark smoke enveloped the printed manuscript, becoming the cover. A single human eye, his own, peeked out of the darkness. With the cover art finalized, title placed, his name etched in the usual spot at the top, the book was now complete as if it had just come off the printer at a publishing house.

11

Four days later, news reporters swarmed Sorrel's estate.

"This is Catherine Jones from BIG1 news, reporting live from the newly acquired estate of famed horror writer, Sorrel, who simply went by that name on his books. No one has seen or heard from the Frenchman since staying the night here four nights ago.

"When the employees arrived three days ago that morning, they claim Sorrel wasn't to be found. At that point, there was nothing to report, so they worked and waited for their boss to arrive. When he didn't, after numerous attempts to reach him, they contacted the police. If anyone knows the whereabouts of Sorrel, please contact authorities at the number on the bottom of the screen.

"Adding to the mystery, one employee here found a novel with Sorrel's name on it. His agent claims he didn't know Sorrel was working on another book, let alone one that was ready for release."

The reporter opened the novel and showed the first few pages into the camera.

"As you can see, there is no copyright page, so no one knows who had printed this book. Based on the success of

Sorrel's last novel, I'm sure the battle over rights to publish more copies of this book will turn ugly. For now, we'll have to wait and see if Sorrel appears or who will be the lucky publisher to print what may be his last book."

The reporter closed the book and showed the cover to the camera. As the camera zoomed in, out of the smokey-printed cover peeked a single human eye—Sorrel's.

"The name of the book," the reporter continued, "Where Did They Come From?"

Sorrel blinked.

1

I used to believe I was unique. By unique, I mean there wasn't another me in the universe. Of course, this included the entire planet Earth and all of its subdivisions: the continent, country, state, city—hell, even the same block or immediate vicinity where I was at any given moment. But not anymore.

No, I learned something that I wish I never pursued. However, it was one of those things I had to know. A quest that had originated in my soul as if it itself needed to know. And what we sought wasn't unique to us by any means. Many a person had pondered exactly or damned near what my soul and I had questioned: Are we unique in the world?

Now, you might be saying to yourself, "Of course everyone is unique. You would have to be a fool to think otherwise."

A fool indeed. My soul and I should have left it alone. In the grand scheme of things, who cared whether we were unique or not. Some things are not to be messed with. Not every inquiry needs answering. This one should have remained unanswered.

Unfortunately, I found a way of answering it.

Before we get to that, I should explain that I never questioned whether we were unique *physically*. That goes without saying. I can't even say with a clear conscious that we all have a head, torso, two arms, and two legs. Truth be told, we all don't. Not everyone has the internal plumbing they should and some have a little extra. However, I will concede that the human form usually consists of those things.

Regrettably, what I had set out to know was whether my soul, spirit if you rather, was unique.

You are probably wondering how does one go about answering something as absurd as that? Absurd, indeed. I almost gave up on the undiscoverable—until I discovered it. As I said earlier, I found a way of answering, irrefutably, that question. I won't bore you with the details, let me just say I am a scientist who happened to stumble upon the soul during one of my experiments.

I must warn you, right now, that you may find my experiments unorthodox and gruesome. In my defense, they had to be. There was no way I would find the soul through x-rays or weighing the body before and after death, as MacDougall had done at the turn of the twentieth century, or by any other unobtrusive methods. Nor could I rely on beliefs or faiths of any kind. Believing something is true or having confidence in nothing more than an opinion is worthless when it comes to proving something. Arguing would never end and if we ever reached the end, neither of us would have anything to stand on. It was of the utmost importance that I find the substance of such things—the evidence of things unseen.

Most had assumed that the soul couldn't be seen and, therefore, finding something invisible was unachievable and a waste of time. They had forgotten about basic things and forces we cannot see that are there: air, oxygen, and gravity to name a few of a myriad of things that we cannot see but are at work every day in our lives.

My experiments had to wander in the human substance to find it. Such experimentation is always messy, yet, a small price to endure in such an important quest in finding the human soul.

Now, time was saved by a not-so-scientific process of elimination. Finding the soul in the feet, legs, arms, or hands were doubtful, so I avoided searching them. The torso held possibilities, in particular, the heart, but wandering around in there increased the risk of death in my subjects.

Sexual organs of the crotch weren't entirely off my radar, in fact, with the man's sperm holding half of life's DNA and the women's eggs the other half, this life-producing cocktail couldn't be ignored.

For a time I ignored it and concentrated my efforts where most would—the brain. Exploration here carried with it life-threatening risks as the heart but had to be done.

Of course, to find the soul, I had to search inside living beings with the soul active and at work. This energy in motion, I hoped, would somehow display its power, wanting to be found, signaling to me its exact location.

One of my greatest fears was that the soul didn't reside in a particular location but instead wandered inside the body like a fish inside a tank. If true, opening the body at just the right time and finding it would be a real crapshoot. It was very possible the soul would flee my entrance point in self-preservation or to avoid unintentional leaking out of the body, leaving the person soulless.

Other fears haunted me. What if the soul flowed within

the blood? Cuts and other unwanted entries making it possible for some of the soul to be lost. Bleeding out equaled losing one's soul and possibly death.

Finding the soul *as is* would take a miracle and trying to find it within the blood unlikely if not impossible. As would if it somehow existed within our breath.

Don't laugh. I do not consider the Bible the authority on such matters, nor any other religious text. However, I must consider what the Bible has to say. When it contains a recording in it that God is a spirit, it seemed prudent to at least see what it and its other supporting study works, such as the concordance and lexicon, have to say on the matter. After all, who knows for sure whether man came before language communication or whether man came into being already equipped with language, but had to resort to symbols and drawings before alphabets ushered in the written word.

If God is a spirit and Adam was made in his image, inclusive of a spirit, then why is it unreasonable to reason that if God spoke creation into existence that he had also breathed language into Adam when he had created him? Most Christians don't even know God is described as a spirit, let alone question how did Adam talk to God exactly?

I'll admit, maybe it wasn't verbal, but a spirit-to-spirit connection and God spoke with his own spirit as it had moved over Earth to create it.

This is from a Christian perspective, but there are others. Not all of which refer to a spirit, but those that do are eerily consistent that it is nothing more than a wind or a breath.

Still, there existed a more troubling scenario. What if the soul didn't exist at all and I had wasted my time along with human resources?

Then, to my relief,—I saw it—the substance of the soul.

You're probably wondering how it happened—so I'll tell you.

2

Every morning, I wake up to a view of the Baltic Sea outside my bedroom window. For time sake, life had treated me well. With that preferential treatment, I had purchased a secluded property in Skatre, Latvia.

I didn't always have a view of the sea. When I first moved in, trees between the beach and my home had blocked the Baltic. That was until I had a number of them cut down. Needless to say, I caught hell for it and promised to grow them back. That was fifteen years ago and, now, I'm middle-aged. And I never did plant one damn seed.

Life was good. I wasn't married. Never had any children. Nor wanted either. Honestly, it's a big reason why I accumulated the wealth I had so quickly.

My next big purchase was a boat. Yes, even before a car. Although life wiped my ass with a golden cloth and I had the money to buy one, I lived there three years before I bought a wheeled vehicle. I vowed to live off the land. Do my own fishing. Grow my own crops. Well and purify my own water.

I failed miserably. However, one good thing came from that failure. I lost a lot of weight and was in the best shape of my life.

There are ten ports in Latvia: three hug the coasts of the Baltic Sea and the other seven are spread out along the southern half of the Gulf of Riga. The closest is Liepāja, five miles away, and the farthest is Salacgrīva, four hours away. That's where I met him.

Once a month, I visit a port. Outside of the frequency, my visits are purposefully un-patternable. Although it was early in the month, it was time to head out again and Salacgrīva was next in my seemingly-random cycle.

Four hours is a long drive for anyone, let alone for a man of leisure as myself. However, I never minded the trip. Heading inland, east along A9, wasn't my favorite, but there was no way of avoiding it. A stop at Riga, which has our largest port, couldn't be avoided either. A refill of some of that Russian gas and a meal filling my stomach were necessities before heading north up E67 where the Baltic peeks at me through trees now and again. An hour and a half later was usually enough time for the buzz from the beers I had drunk along with my meal to stop buzzing.

Standing at a distance away from the port, I pulled a flask out of my jacket pocket. A sip of Black Balsam warmed my throat as I watched a cargo ship enter the "Mouth of Salaca."

All I can say about the drink is that I was introduced to it the first year I had moved to Skatre. Some kind of sickness kicked my ass into bed and let me lie there to die. Of all people, my mail carrier had noticed the pile-up in my box and entered the house to check on me. He found me lying face down on the bed. I don't remember anything from that encounter, only what he had shared with me afterward. Apparently, he sat me up and poured a swig of the balsam down my throat and left me to die. That's right, no doctor or anything. Within a few days, I was back on my feet again. When I had asked about a doctor, he said, "No need. I knew the balsam would make you well again."

From that moment on, not once did I ever give him a

hard time about late or jumbled up mail

A bug's gnawing at my insides again. There was no way I was drinking the stuff while driving. Hell, I didn't want to drink it now. But with what I had to do, I had to kill the bug inside me.

Now, I know you're wondering what did I have to do that was so darn important to make such a long drive and be out when I'm not feeling good? Well, I'll tell you. The pursuit of *truth* had spurred me on. And no, it couldn't wait. Time doesn't wait for anyone and truth only tells the truth when it's good and ready, so you have to be around for it to hear it.

Now, back to *him*—the man I had met. He was working on a cargo ship when I had first seen him. A force deeper than attraction had drawn me to him. The whole experience was unusual. Not just on these trips to ports, but in my life. Never had I felt such an internal draw to another human being. Which is saying a lot, because there are some women out there with the power to reduce me down to an infant state, complete with drool and soiling myself. Not that I would mind going to bed with them every night if I could keep up. Nor waking next to them every morning. As long as they went their own way during the day, left me to my business, and my assets in my sole name, women and I got along fine.

All of that to say I'm not a homosexual, nor ever would be. No, what had gripped me seeing that man was something spiritual. From first glimpse, that man's spirit agreed with mine. A connection that I would later learn went deeper than linking.

3

The cargo ship remained in port for two days, which meant the man stayed at a hotel in Salacgrīva. The closest one to the port, I might add — no more than a ten-minute walk. Unable to do what I had initially set out to do, I never returned home and booked a room in the same hotel as the man—the Brize, viesnica-pansionats, Maksis in Deli.

Don't be fooled. It sounds fancy, but it's not. It's not a dump either. And not that big. So I ran into him in the hall.

First words out of his mouth told me he was Russian. To be clear, I am Latvian, born and raised. Not that it makes a difference, but please keep it in mind.

After some friendly chit-chat, I introduced myself as Raimonds and he as Kazimir. He wouldn't let go of my hand. Perhaps he had also felt the current flowing through us, not only through our handshake but through our eye contact.

My eyes broke the connection to look down at our clasped hands. When Kazimir realized what was happening, he pulled his hand away and said, "Oh, I'm not…" and I quickly agreed, "Me neither."

A sigh of relief expelled out of him, unashamedly.

"I know—right," I said.

Catching his breath, he said, "Whew, what a relief."

"You, uh, ..." My finger wiggled between us like a squirming worm.

"Yeah." Kazimir cocked his head. "That was intense."

"That's it. When did you first notice it?"

"Right away, but it felt wrong, so I tried hiding it."

Of course, I couldn't tell him that I first noticed it at a greater distance while watching him work on the ship. Thankfully, he never knew to ask.

"What is it?" Kazimir asked.

"I'm not sure. But how about a drink," I offered.

"I was thinking the same thing."

I knew of a place nearby—nearby a relevant term in Salacgrīva.

We ended up at a bar he had been to before. When I had asked him how many times he had been into port, he answered, "Eleven."

Instead of feeling relief in anticipating a much lower number, I felt confused. Eleven is a large number. So how did we miss each other?

"My world," I said. "Eleven."

"Yep," Kazimir confirmed. "I keep track of every port I visit and how many times. Funny, I've never seen you in these parts before."

"It's been a month or two."

He gulped his beer and leaned over the table and whispered, "Do you think if we had met earlier that what happened back at the hotel still would have happened?"

"I don't know. I'm not quite sure what this is, but I want to find out."

A bellowed laugh shook the Russian; beer nearly spilled out of his mug. "Good thing we know what this isn't, huh?"

Confirmation of my sexual preference was behind that question.

"No need to play straight-edge with me," I said. "Latvians are straighter than any Russian."

Pride kept me upright—so did stupidity—as I braced

myself for a club upside the head.

Awkward moments passed until I finally said, "Well?"

"Well, what?" Kazimir said right before gulping his beer.

"Aren't you going to hit me?"

"For that? *Na*. Besides—it would be like hitting myself."

A choke seized my dry throat since I hadn't taken a drink since making the comment. His words choked me as if I had spoken them myself. What could he mean?

"What do you mean?" I asked.

"About what?"

"About hitting *me* would be like hitting yourself."

"Yeah, that's right," he said, then drank more brew.

"I mean why do you feel that way?" I clarified. "We just met."

As Kazimir lowered the mug, thought occupied him. When it registered, he said, "Funny. It doesn't feel that way."

At first, I stared at him. It wasn't funny. Then, I downed the rest of my beer and banged the empty mug on the table.

"You know what?" I said. "I don't feel that way either. And don't have a clue as to why."

The last frothy remnant of beer in Kazimir's mug disappeared and he, too, banged his mug on the table.

No one had said, "Simon says," and no one at this table was named Simon. It could have been nothing more than monkey see-monkey do, but Kazimir was far from man's evolution beginnings. Perhaps his copying stemmed from something deeper—a connection within our blood—like a brother.

A nervous excitement pulsed through me as if my nervous system had been rewired and rigged like a low-yield electric fence. Buzzing rattled me slightly as I thought about what I had said—*a connection within our blood—like a brother*.

Was it possible? Not in a shared-mother sense. Something beyond the physical. Or it seemed that way to us, but maybe it wasn't.

I had to get doing what had brought me up here in the

first place.

4

The next morning, I felt good. Between the Black Balsam, the energy from meeting Kazimir, and, who knows, maybe the beer and dinner, had killed the bug inside me. All that was left to do now was shit it out of me.

On the toilet, I reminded myself of what I had plotted last night for today. There wasn't any use in dragging this out any longer. Swift action had always worked before and my unplanned postponement yesterday had thrown me off. Not today. It's back to the business of why I had driven up here in the first place.

Resolute and the bug presumably out of me, I stood and wiped. On my way to the sink, a knock sounded on my door.

"I might be staying another night," I yelled out.

No one answered—only knocking.

Drying my hands, I went to the door. "I said…"

"Raimonds, it's Kazimir."

Only he had said Raimond, or probably thought Raymond, leaving off the *s* as most do.

I unlocked the door and Kazimir barged in.

Embarrassed by the stench I had made, I gestured

40

apologetically.

"I'm sorry, Kazimir," I began.

The Russian interrupted me. "Get some clothes on and let's go. You have to see this."

"See what?"

"Come. I'll tell you on the way."

After I got dressed, the Russian led the way and rambled on, telling me he had returned to the ship to explain why there was a particular cargo on board to the Salacgrīva Port Authority. Another vessel had docked near his and he had seen a man who had caused the same unexplainable connection that he had experienced with me yesterday. While it was happening, he said he almost botched-up the explanation to the port authority, which could have gotten him fired and the cargo shippers in a lot of trouble.

When we arrived at the dock, the Russian smiled and pointed out the man he had seen earlier.

The man was just coming onto land. An awareness seemed to wobble his eyeballs in their sockets like a settling compass. They polarized when he looked at us. Kazimir and I were staring back. All three of us settled in place.

Someone coming off the ship knocked into the back of the man, having a few choice words for him to get out of the way, but they never registered past the man's concentration on us.

As if our brother had returned from war, Kazimir and I trotted toward him. Counterintuitive, the man ran toward us—two total strangers. The whole thing inexplicable.

When we all arrived at the meeting place, we didn't hug or anything goofy like that. The man's eyes alternated between staring at Kazimir, then me—back-and-forth. It was easier for Kazimir and I only having one person to look at.

The Russian reached out a hand. "The name's Kazimir."

"*Ah*, Russian, eh," the man said. "Berhan."

They shook hands for a long time, apparently having a connective-experience.

When they were done, I extended a hand. "Berhan—Raimonds."

We, too, had that meaningful connectivity.

"I can't place where you are from, Raimonds," the man said.

"I'm local."

"A local, eh. You must show me around."

Another unplanned delay in my plans had me seething.

"You'll be disappointed," I said. "There are parts of the area Canadians aren't allowed."

"Funny," Berhan said. "I like that."

"When do you ship off?" Kazimir asked.

"We're not sure," Berhan answered. "We might ship off tonight, but my guess is it will be tomorrow morning."

"Me, too," Kazimir offered. "Port got to our ship faster than expected."

Hearing that made me boil more. I was running out of time. Then, I remembered my words yesterday about a connection in our blood—like brothers and a glimmer of light presented itself within my darkness. Perhaps, this could turn into one of the best trips I've ever had to any port.

"How about a beer?" I heard myself saying. "And a room? Let's get your room first."

After getting Berhan checked into a room, we went to the same place that Kazimir and I had last night. We even ended up sitting at the same table—Kazimir and I sat in the same seats—with the third wheel sitting between us.

Nearly drunk, the Canadian couldn't contain it anymore and asked, "What happened back there? I mean, when we first met."

I looked at Kazimir and asked, "Do you wish to start or should I?"

5

The more confused Kazimir and Berhan became the more drunk they had become. Festivities had started that morning, so it wasn't late, not even dinner time. We had graduated from beer to the harder stuff.

I, on the other hand, had slowed my alcohol consumption quite a bit. At first, they noticed and ragged me about it. Then they lost count—both mine and theirs. This was my chance.

Until I noticed something. It was strange I hadn't seen it before. Watching the men move, their mannerisms, they were nearly identical. I started observing my own, which was difficult to do and maintain any normalcy. It's only natural for someone to become a little reserved when being watched. I fought it off, playing tag with myself, trying to catch myself off-guard for a scientific observance to compare to the other guys. It was impossible. How does one surprise themselves?

My eyes made impromptu checks of myself only to be caught in the act as my mind had already calculated when my eye's intentions would act. To combat this, whatever I was doing at the time, I froze in place so I could see hand gestures, movements, how I sat, how I reacted. Physically, we moved damned near the same—a Latvian, Russian, and Canadian—born to different parents and unrelated.

The Canadian came off with something that I would say and, to my surprise, the Russian said, "I've used that before."

So I started paying attention to words and phrases. Dialect made this most difficult, especially with the Russian *V* and *W* exchange, the Candian's *eh*, and even my own wordship. Yet, underneath the sounds uttered the same verbiage.

Hell, maybe *I* was drunk. Normally, my tolerance to alcohol tolerated nearly any kind of spirit and in mass quantity. Perhaps it was *I* who had lost count.

No one would ever guess that Kazimir and Berhan were the deep-thinking, what-the-hell-is-the-meaning-of-life types under their physical forms as seamen. But I could see it— sense it that they, too, were watching, listening, comparing.

Yes, even in their drunken state.

Every hour that passed meant less of a chance of me accomplishing what I had come here to do.

"Let's get out of here," Berhan said. "I can hold my liquor, but I'll be sicker than an unborn infant puking out of its mother, making the mother puke come ship-off."

A surprise opening of opportunity had presented itself.

"Rough seas forecasted tomorrow," Kazimir said. "If we stay here, I'll just keep drinking and end up reddening the sea myself."

"One more for the road," I suggested. "I'll settle up as I fetch them."

Neither opposed, so instead of waiting on our server, I walked up to the bar and ordered three more drinks—the hard stuff—mine watered-down. One-by-one, as they were set on the bar and the bartender poured the next, I dabbed into theirs another concoction I had brought with me to port. Not the Black Balsam. No, this I had created in my spare time years ago and had perfected to achieve the desired effect. My sprinkles had to be accurate to ensure that they should make it back to the hotel without me having to carry them.

After drinking our drinks, we walked back toward the hotel. While passing a white church, the cross perched on the steeple spoke to me. Don't laugh. People hear inanimate objects talk all the time. Telling them they are loved, hated, what they must do, and in the name of who. The never-lived can speak, yet the dead who have lived cannot is pure foolishness.

I believe they both can communicate with the living. Inanimate objects were conceived in the mind of someone living. Built by living hands, for dead hands can't build.

Or can they? Dead hands are usually depicted as destroyers. One's soul went into making such things; a part of the creator infused into what they had made.

"My, Lord," I said aloud.

Considering the church in front of us, Kazimir and Berhan didn't think much of my words—if at all—for they didn't say anything.

But the cross on the steeple did. At least to me. So, I listened.

Like most things in life, when broken down to their basic element, the direction was simple. My original plan that had brought me to port simply had to be multiplied by two.

No one ever knows for sure if their intuition is accurate or not, but the cross had ensured me it was. It was the first time in my middle-of-the-road life that a religious emblem had provided me peace.

6

Instead of us going to our hotel rooms, we all got into my car. Berhan needed some help, but once he and Kazimir had slid into the back seat, both men were out. My concoction that I had slipped into their drinks had worked beautifully.

The four-hour drive back to my house in Skatre went without incident. Traffic was light and the darkness calmed me. Within that calm, adrenaline kept me awake. Outside of stopping once for gas and a coffee, I drove straight through.

A *twofer* the cross had told me in a more magisterial voice that had seemed to twang like vibrating metal, which the cross was made of.

We arrived. Instead of going to work right away, I fed them more of my concoction so I could have a few hours of sleep. They were fed more than enough as to not wake before me. My head rested on my familiar pillow and, almost instantly, I faded out—asleep.

The rising sun peeked over the Baltic waters and into my bedroom. It kissed me warmly on the cheek. As I sat up to take in her beauty, her radiance greeted me a good morning. I took it as a sign it was going to be a good day.

46

After cleaning myself up after a night filled with possibilities, I made myself a hot breakfast of eggs, sausage patties, and some coffee. Expectations filled my heart and mind as I ate—while the Russian and Canadian slept.

At least I assumed they were still asleep because I never checked in on them. My assumption could be described as more than that because, let's just say, there was a certainty about it. I had felt it as if I were asleep myself.

Done eating, I assumed now might be the time before they awoke. Preparations weren't taxing by any stretch of the imagination but still needed to be done.

Leaving the pan on the stove and the rest of the dishes in the sink, I checked in on them. They were still asleep.

Having, I figured, maybe another hour or two, I went out to the porch and picked up the morning paper. A quick skim of the Local and Financial sections gave me enough time to finish my coffee.

Satisfied and ready to start, I opened the pantry door. Simply sliding a few canned goods stacked near a corner out of the way and a two-finger-twist of a latch and the pantry shelving unlocked. It opened like a door and I descended the stairs into a separate cellar tucked below the center of the house within the everyday cellar that ran around its perimeter—a cellar within a cellar.

Now it wasn't big, as you can imagine, but big enough for what I had done there the last fifteen years.

From what I could find out, the secret room had acted as a slave hideaway as ships came into port. People can get a little touchy about such subjects, but truth be told, as technology brought about faster means of travel and wars and business scattered people to all parts of the Earth, we're all a mixed breed of sorts—part this and part that.

Based on the condition of the pantry shelving, there's no doubt in my mind it's the original, which tells me no one outside of staying there had ever learned of the hideaway.

Now, I'm an old recluse, so take this with a grain of salt from the Baltic itself, but no one has ever returned to see it, so I'm not sure how many had come through. It's understandable why someone who had stayed there wouldn't want to visit such a painful memory, although there are people today who want to see how far they have come from lows in their life.

I must say, that if such a person ever visited and wanted to see it, I would have to deny them. For the room has changed to the point they wouldn't recognize it. Structurally it's the same, but I have things down there that they may find suspicious. That would be bad for them. So, you see, I would be protecting them by not showing them the room.

Things like instruments, which may someday allow me to see the wind. Inventors of such gadgets created them for practical uses, mainly scientific and weather-related observations. Scientists and meteorologists have tools at their disposal that allow them to learn and even predict outcomes based on the movement of the wind. I doubt any of the creators or users of such instruments ever thought of using them for my purpose: to see a living soul.

Of all things, a word: *spirit*, had brought me to this connection—a pattern I couldn't ignore. *Pneúma* in Greek, *rúach* in Hebrew, *esprit* in French, *garu* in Latvian, or many other words for *spirit* in a number of languages all describe an elusive *wind* or *breath*. Perhaps the Bosnian *duh* is best of all *spirit* equivalents.

I'm not here to argue whether the soul and spirit are different things. Defined, they are synonyms. By religious groups, they may be interpreted differently, the spirit is our true self that moves out of the body and on into eternity, or perhaps reincarnated into another body, and all other sorts of scenarios, while the soul is our mannerisms.

Under the religious distinction, if I do see something, how will I know whether I'm looking at the spirit or the soul? As a scientist, I'm abiding by the definition that they are one-in-the-same. The only way I would change my mind is if by chance I happen to see two distinct winds within the same body.

Wind is nothing more than a movement of air. Breath is nothing more than air moving into and out of the body. So, if our soul, or spirit, amounted to air movement, then why couldn't I use existing instruments to see it?

The instruments *as is* hadn't worked—I never saw a soul—and some of them could be tossed out of the mix. For example, thermometers measure air temperature, which is useless in my endeavor. If a soul or spirit contains any thermal or cooling properties at all, no one knows precisely how much accounts for the average human temperature of ninety-eight point six degrees.

Anemometers gauge wind speeds. Barometers measure air pressure. Wind vanes determine which direction the wind is blowing.

Although these instruments couldn't magnify the spirit on their own, I had grown confident I was on the right track.

As a scientist, it is my job to think through things as thoroughly as possible. In doing so, I couldn't ignore my own eyes. After all, they were the instruments in my body that would either allow me or not to see what I sought.

The human eye can only see within a narrow range of the color spectrum. People need help seeing anything outside of this range by using enhancers, such as glasses, magnifying glasses, infra-red for enhanced night vision, binoculars, X-rays, telescopes, bionic eyes, and the list continues to grow as new vision enhancers are created.

Years ago, while at the checkout at a supermarket, the barcode scanner caught my attention. Complex in their own right, in the simplest of terms, scanners decode barcodes, which are always black and white, by differentiating between those two colors. White reflects more light, while black absorbs more light. With this knowledge, I found my eyes became more sensitive to light the more time I spent in my dark basement and allowed them to adjust.

Achieving optimal lighting became critical to my success. Testing the lighting in my home by drawing curtains to different points on well-lit windows and those not-so-well-lit and then observing when could I see the most particles in the air and when I couldn't was more valuable than you can imagine. Though I couldn't see the particles under certain conditions, they were still there. We live like this every day. So, if the spirit does exist and we can't see it, then how do I create an environment to see it?

So far, modifications to existing instruments deemed useful and combining those instruments to make my own wind-breath-detecting-camera hasn't produced any results.

However, concrete, scientific reasons, too burdensome to explain, had me believing I was close.

7

Of everything I explained, all important, keep this in mind above all others: the lens and the processes behind it are of the utmost importance. For it was the lense that must handle a broadened color spectrum and optimal lighting to detect the spirit-wind. The image needed to be received and processed in a way that it could be understood.

In the most unscientific way, I essentially described the human eye. Some people have eyes that do exactly what I had described. Some may refer to what they see as spirits or souls, but a more common term might be one that you can relate: *ghosts*.

Commonly, ghosts are witnessed outside of their bodies and said to be captured by regular cameras and video recorders. I'm sure many are hoaxes, but who am I to judge; I don't have that ability. Besides, I'm interested in capturing the soul at work while still *inside* the body—not out.

When I was about to give up on trying to produce such a device, which others have claimed they have, an idea had come to me. Rather than create such a device, why don't I use what's at my disposal.

A week ago, I drove to the Roja Port and met a woman,

who had seen me and in no uncertain terms told me she was horny and wanted me. This had never happened to me before—not so bluntly. It was the easiest luck I ever had sneak up on me and yell, *Boo!*

A little frightened, there was no way I was showing her where I lived and I doubt she meant, "Drive me two and a half hours and then take me."

It was a safe assumption. So, rather than lose her, I took her to the closest hotel I could find.

Little did she know, she was making this trip one of the easiest I ever had in fifteen years.

An entire day had passed. I never needed water and food so desperately in my life. Dehydrated and famished came close to describing my condition but it felt worse. Ten pounds of me in the form of sweat had been left that August day in room 3C. For all I know, probably still there.

After ordering room service, two carts rolled into the room with an ungodly amount of food and drink for two people. When we had finished, she wanted to go again.

I asked her when was the last time someone just held her and she said it had been quite a while. In self-defense, I offered. Unconvinced, she started up again. I grabbed her head with both hands, looked into her eyes, and told I loved her. It was a lie, of course, but a man will do anything to keep from being ripped apart.

She laid next to me and told me her life story. It was quite entertaining. Especially, when she had said that she could see ghosts.

As much as she wanted to keep returning to past loves lost and hardships, I kept bringing her back to that gift.

Convinced her gift was real, I had asked her if she wanted to come and stay at my place and I'd take her back to port before her ship shoved off.

I knew she would say yes and did, so I took her home— knowing damn well she would miss her voyage and that I wouldn't be in Roja until my next scheduled rotation.

8

Banging sounded from upstairs. Kazimir, the Russian, and Berhan, the Canadian, had awakened. Perfect timing, because everything was set up and ready to go.

After I trodded up two floors from the basement to a bedroom, Berhan was wiggling on the bed; zip-ties around his wrists and ankles held him down. I heard Kazimir struggling to free himself in the other bedroom.

No one can say I am a terrible host. Comfort is important to me and I assume it is for others. That's why I had assisted them up a flight of stairs to a bedroom; no different than putting a sleepy child to bed.

I administered more of my sleeping concoction into Berhan, who strained to free himself until the potion took effect.

As I entered Kazimir's room, he stopped wiggling; his neck craned to look at me.

Now came the hard part—even harder than putting them to bed. This was where another one of my concoctions had come in handy.

With the paralyzer administered and a half-an-hour elapsed,

I poked the same used needle into Kazimir all over his body to ensure the potion had taken effect. Drops of blood beaded where the tip of the needle had penetrated. Not always in science, but in this instance, a nonreaction was a good thing.

After fifteen years of not getting caught—not even one inquiry into any of the missing persons—I had learned every precaution, ensuring this streak remained intact.

Once I'm satisfied the subject was alive and unable to scream, I wheelchaired them over to the dumbwaiter, stuffed them inside, pressed the button, and lowered them into the basement.

It's a pain for me, but I appreciate those who had helped me in my work. All I ask is that they reciprocate with the same courtesy.

With Kazimir strapped onto what amounted to a tilting operation table, my work continued as I waited for the paralyzer to wear off.

Down here, he could scream all he wanted because the basement had been soundproofed. I only tested it once, years ago, when I had a real screamer. Man did this teenage girl have high hopes of an easy life, as well as one hell of a pair of lungs.

While she screamed all of the hate, crushing disappointment, and fear I've never heard before or since, I had stepped out of the pantry and into the kitchen and heard nothing. The same at the front and back doors, on the porch, and taking a lap around the house—I couldn't hear her screams.

Flanking Kazimir on both sides were wind-detecting contraptions attached to the wall that swiveled on brackets like turnable speakers. Another overhead stared down at him from the ceiling like the eye of God, but it wasn't on. Wires, attached to the walls and ceiling, extended to two powerfully-modified computers with large screens—my workstation—set up to record both sound and picture for the entire procedure; one equipped with infrared and other filtered views to capture the soul and another for general recording. Of the two, the latter must work flawlessly in order to obtain the first video evidence in the history of man of a soul housed within a living body.

As I had stated before, the lens was the most important. Second, having a processor that could handle what the lens saw. Without question, the computers could handle such a task, but there was a tried-and-true processor I didn't feel needed improvement—once I figured it out.

No question, Kazimir wanted to scream. His gaped mouth and strained neck went through the motions but didn't produce a sound, not even a squeak. And despite the speakers reflecting in his glossy eyes, they were preoccupied elsewhere—not on the speakers. No, they took in my revelation, tried-and-true since perhaps Adam and Eve, both of whom may have gained gifted eyes to see that old serpent the devil after their fall in the garden. Perched on top of a tripod in front of him was the sexually ravenous woman's head.

Now, I may not know the name of the woman, whose sexual stamina had nearly killed me, nor all of the other names to give her and others proper credit, but I still can see their faces. Well, most of them anyway. But know this, her name would top all others, for she was the first subject to elevate to a higher-calling, a tool, that after revolutionizing my methods, might be what I had been missing all of these years in searching for the spirit within the body.

I remember holding her in my arms and asking when she looked at someone, like me, could she see the soul—my soul? Her answer of *"no"* disappointed me, but her explanation made total sense. *"The flesh of the body concealed it,"* she had said and I believed her. It justified my reasons for using live subjects and opening them up. A confirmation to continue with such research methods in hopes of one day seeing a human spirit.

Wires vined up the tripod, up and over the back and

sides of her head like hair, and their ends disappeared into her exposed brain. If she really could see ghosts outside of the body when she was alive, I had everything riding on her gifted eyes—my lenses—seeing the soul inside an opened body and her brain—my key image decoder—processing what her eyes were about to see.

9

It's been almost a week since I detached her head from her body, so I hoped her functions still functioned. Everything counted on it. Otherwise, it was back to the drawing board.

The head had been partially cryonically preserved. Partly, because I had no intention of storing it long-term, so the blood and fluids weren't removed as was generally practiced in cryonics. Besides, replacing the fluids, even in a single body part—the head—would have been a royal pain. So, storage entailed careful temperature control as to not freeze or damage the cells.

It should be noted, my method of storing deviated in another way. The temperature inside my canister was thirty-one-point-five degrees Fahrenheit, balmy when compared to the usual two-hundred and forty degrees Fahrenheit below zero for cryonic storage, but cold-enough to preserve the head for one week. I had also filled the bottom of the canister with her blood and set her head in upside-down so the exposed brain could drink and, hopefully, remain alive. Without a living heart to pump blood to the brain to oxygenize it, since the head had been detached from the body, I hoped submersing it in blood would keep the brain fed while buying me time.

Special care was taken to ensure the blood-level remained eye-level and that the head remained upright. Keeping the eyes clean was of utmost importance.

When science was ready to be known it almost always showed itself. If you don't believe me, all you have to do is research how many discoveries were discovered by accident and you'd see what I mean. Scientists, any sex, any age, can be the proudest of all people and in error of puffing themselves up with air they never produced. For failed science had a knack of popping at the most inopportune time and blowing that same air back in their faces.

I would not make the same mistake. And I didn't. When I had checked the infrared computer screen, live images of Kazimir, strapped to the tilted operating table, had successfully displayed on its screen. My unorthodox way of relaying and processing information had worked. Which meant the connectivity between the sex-fiend's working eyes and brain and the wires connected to the computer had operated beautifully despite using organic and nonorganic materials.

Although I had kept myself in check, my expectations were another matter. I had no control over them. My puffed up air floated them to heights I worried couldn't be achieved. Most of all, the elevation scared me. Falling from such a height would only mean one thing—my own death.

A man can die without physically dying. For fifteen years, I have successfully avoided that one thing to live to see the day when I would become the first human being ever to see, record, and show the world what the soul looked like at work within a living body. Without further ado, it was time to see whether my hard work and risk-taking had paid off.

Already dressed in scrubs, I slipped the cap over my head, donned the goggles, and placed the mask over my mouth and nose. There was no use in washing my hands, but I did put on surgical gloves.

The cart squealed as I rolled it beside the operating table.

Kazimir's eyes widened, for the surgical instruments on the cart weren't the cleanest, but still serviceable. I did my best to console him as I leveled the operating table, spun it around so his head faced the woman's head on the tripod, and locked it in place.

I picked up the blood-crusted scalpel, the only I had, gently lifted the Russian's head and made an incision at the hairline above the neck. With blood flowing, I was on the clock, so when I tossed the red-coated scalpel on the other instruments on the cart, it clanked. Similar to an hourglass, which kept time as long as the sand flowed, as long as Kazimir's blood spilled, I had time.

I felt the tips of my gloved fingers insert through the gash in the back of his head. The squishy sound of my fingers separating the scalp from the cranium wasn't something I ever got used to, even as many times I had done it.

With my fingers inserted up to the thumb, I grabbed a handful of scalp and hair and yanked until the entire skull was exposed; Kazimir's own hair was in his face.

Keep in mind, my paralyzer concoction reduced the pain but was no match against such trauma and painkillers had always made me feel leery that it would somehow reduce my chances of seeing the soul. So, my subjects, I'm afraid to say, had to experience the pain that I accepted responsibility for. This went against my view of comfort, but science held more significance than any of us.

There wasn't enough time to drill boreholes into Kazimir's cranium first before connecting them with a bone saw, so, right away, retrieving the saw from the cart without blocking my lover's view, I sawed a crude circle around the cranium.

Next came my favorite part and the moment when I might catch the spirit in action within the human body. My fingers swiveled the cutaway bone, resting on the brain, ever so slightly to loosen the cerebrospinal fluid's hold.

A tip of a screwdriver, wedged into the saw line, created

enough space for my finger. As I pulled, the cranium bone un-suctioned off the brain. When I discarded it onto the floor, it sounded like a gourd hitting the kitchen floor after rolling off the counter.

Checking the infrared monitor—I saw it—the human soul.

10

It amounted to a ghostly energy, a wind, perhaps even God's breath, glowing around the tissue of Kazimir's brain, specifically, the frontal lobe, which housed problem-solving, reasoning, and emotional traits. With Kazimir living his closing moments, this made sense.

Turning my head to look at the brain itself, I saw nothing. When I returned to the infrared computer screen, it was still there—pulsating its ora in a slow, steady rhythm. A glance to the general recording screen, the spirit wasn't there.

I picked up the tripod with the head on it and pointed the woman's gifted eyes on Kazimir's brain. It was if she had bent down herself for a closer look.

My mouth rambled on, more than before, trying to document, verbally, what I saw, how I saw it, and what I thought was happening, including Kazimir's dying—the best I could from an observer's point of view.

Beyond luck, science revealed to me a previous unknown. Soon, mankind would know it, too.

As I watched the infrared screen and the woman's head watched Kazimir's brain, I verbalized every observation that came to mind, no matter how insignificant it seemed.

Suddenly, the soul disappeared into the brain like a water puddle finding cracks in the sidewalk and seeping through.

Without question, the energy dove deeper into the brain and not someplace else. Video evidence would confirm it.

The only explanation I had was that the soul might have gone to the temporal lobe where Kazimir's memories, or life, would flash before his mind's eye before seeing a tunnel of light and, then, slipping into death's darkness.

If, that was how it would go. Science had evidence of such things and, of course, proofs contradicting other supposed proofs.

Observation of Kazimir had lasted a good hour after his death. I never saw the spirit leave his body, then again, it's not like my eyes were glued to the infrared screen the entire time.

I remember I had intended to go back and examine the video frame-by-frame, but I never had the chance.

Like science, there were moments in my life where I believed the soul lived on and other times where I didn't—dead was dead—entirely.

Although I hadn't witnessed Kazimir's spirit leave his body, that day I was a believer, mostly for Kazimir's sake. He deserved it, if for no other reason than his contribution to science and expanding our knowledge of ourselves.

Initially, he was simply to be examined using the woman's gifted eyes. However, new questions had come, which happens so often in science. Especially after experiencing and observing the strange connection between Kazimir, Berhan, and myself. A powerful connection beyond the physical, where our verbal communication and mannerisms from the soul had manifested into the physical.

Curiosity had persuaded me to act. And after all of the pondering, a scientist acts through experiments. Beyond need, I had to know whether Kazimir and Berhan had the same soul. Very soon, I would have to examine myself and see if the three of us all had the same soul or different.

This was where my mind needed to remain open. Maybe all souls appear the same? I had to consider it—and be careful.

But first, Berhan.

I had opened him up in the same fashion as Kazimir. From where I stood, his soul appeared to be identical to Kazimir's on the infrared monitor. It even acted in the same way, pulsating at the frontal lobe before descending into deeper tissue to, I believe, the temporal lobe. Temporary was fitting because Berhan had died shortly after.

11

The buzzer installed in my soundproof basement hadn't rung often over the years but did then. Annoying as an alarm clock chirping in your ear when all you want to do is roll over and fall back to sleep, I was glad it hadn't buzzed often. That day, however, it pleased me it had sounded. Someone was at my front door.

When I had opened the door, a mail carrier, a man, began telling me he would be delivering my mail from now on and wanted to introduce himself.

He stopped there, never saying his name. His eyes studied me. His mouth gaped. No doubt, my scrubs threw him off. And the blood and pulp splattered on them. My grabbing him and pulling into the house had taken him by complete surprise. So did the syringe—before I stuck it into his neck.

Paralysis limped his body, making it seem heavier than it was, but really wasn't. Unconscious, uncooperative weight always seemed that way.

A controlled environment is important in science, so his procedure had gone exactly as Kazimir's and Berhan's.

His soul, visible on the infrared computer screen appeared different. More specifically, shape, color, and size. Even the rhythm it pulsated with was faster than the other two. Age could be a factor, so I mentioned it.

Outliers in any experiment were significant finds, especially when the environment, conditions, and methods were the same. Physically comparable, the mailman was a male and about the same build as Kazimir, Berhan, and myself. To say there wasn't a connection at all between the mailman and I would be an understatement, so the results weren't all that surprising.

Maybe luck had waited to meet me in this life on my last day of living. Better late than never I suppose. Not that I buy into that particular viewpoint. What good is having luck for a short time? Not like others who had met luck a lot earlier in life.

Exhaustion had set in. After already logging a number of intense hours of work on others, getting myself prepped for the observation hadn't come easy. Peeling my scalp back and sawing my own cranium took longer than expected. It hurt—bad!

It wouldn't last long I kept telling myself. Funny how the shorter the time to tolerate something makes a difference in our ability to handle excruciating pain.

Lying on the operating table with my brain exposed, studied by the woman's gifted eyes, I remember seeing my soul in the infrared monitor on the ceiling above me.

It was identical to Kazimir's and Berhan's in every way: appearance, shape, color, size, and pulsation.

The physical appearance and taking into account our similar word-choice—a hint into the brain—and the all-to-mimicking of our mannerisms, my pre-death observation suggested that not all souls are different. In other words, from a human-soul perspective, everyone isn't different or uniquely special like snowflakes.

Of all who had ever lived, who else could say such a

thing—that they have seen their own soul active and at work in their body? Not the woman with the gifted eyes, for I wouldn't allow it. The screen overhead hadn't been rigged up yet for infrared. Nor had my soulmates, because the monitor hadn't been turned on until right before my procedure. I doubt it had any impact on the results.

Perhaps, someone like Jesus, a son or daughter of some higher power had seen their own soul. Not likely—not their *own* soul—if they had one. Perhaps, souls were designated for mankind—not deity. Besides, most out-of-body experiences entailed the spirit looking down on the body—not the other way around.

It didn't matter. On this particular occasion, I had felt lucky. Unlike most religions where miracles were passed down verbally and eventually written, I had lived in a day and age when such things could be captured as evidence. Not that many recorded miracles existed, especially when considering nearly everyone on Earth carries a cell phone with a camera and video recording capability. Thus, my lifelong struggle.

Hoaxes existed in the video world as any other, but not this. Someone will eventually find my work—and our bodies. Undisputable evidence if there ever was. Something world religions and unanswered questions, such as man's beginning, lacked.

Perhaps, a scientist might find these recordings and study what had happened here and take my research further. Scientifically, my hypothesis was far from fact. But every man seemed to contain a soul. All of my subjects, including me, had one. Not all unique, but, possibly, standard-issue-spirits.

Compelling evidence of this is the idea of a soul-mate, which I might add isn't always love between two people. No doubt, proximity plays a significant factor and when soul-mates find each other on this massive planet, most describe a soul-deep connection; the same Kazimir, Berhan, and I had.

More evidence might be when we say a person is a particular *type* of person having common characteristics of others we know. Upbringing, environment, and other factors may play into this *commonality* or is there something deeper—as deep as the soul?

Some people *click* with each other like they've known each other forever. Why? Were they issued the same *type* of spirit?

Where souls and the common characteristics come from, are they entwined in our DNA, and who, if anyone, issues them are anybody's guess. But there just might be select standard-issue-spirits to be divided out among the billions, possibly trillions, who have ever lived.

Is it even possible to have that many unique spirits? Once a person dies, is that particular spirit's uniqueness gone from the world forever? Is the spirit reissued, recycled if you prefer, to maintain that spirit-presence on Earth?

Posthumous notoriety never benefited the deceased, always those living to admire and enjoy the work. There will be critics of my findings, there always are, but so be it.

I remember no longer seeing my soul on the screen above me. It must have descended to my temporal lobe. My observations became difficult to verbalize, but I tried anyway. Moments from my life my brain had captured—the first video, image, and sound recorders in the world—began to play and I knew the end was near. The only question now was whether I would die while the images continued to play or when they stopped, I would die.

I think the former happened to me; the images an entrancing lullaby powerful enough to put me to sleep for good.

With my soul, presumably, in my frontal lobe, all of those unanswered questions had drifted away. Otherwise, I would have found it hard to let go of life.

Truth be told, it's impossible for me or anyone to *hold* onto life. When it leaves, it leaves, resulting in death.

Life had left and I was dead.

Now, I know you're asking yourself, if I had died in my basement, then how am I telling you this story?

Could it be that my spirit had been reissued into you?

VACATION'S END

1

Blood pumped through Ramsey's and Blaire's pounding hearts as they made love. Sweat dripped from his face onto her's as he stared at her beauty. He was close—he could feel it. Her green eyes penetrated his and beyond. She felt close, too. Barely able to breathe, they made sounds indistinguishable between pleasure and pain. Their bodies were under great strain. His heart felt as if it might burst out of his chest and enter her's in a literal giving of the heart. An involuntary holding in of breaths as he worked popped veins in his forehead and turned his skin red. Beads of her husband's sweat fell on her face like a beginning rain. She didn't care. Grunting like animals, they ground on each other. Her toes curled as she whimpered and he growled as they climaxed together.

It hadn't always happened that way, but this time it had. Euphoric sensations tingled their bodies with shivering and uncontrollable reactions not always felt after sex.

Ramsey collapsed on his wife and she caressed his head and body everywhere her hands could reach. Their sweaty bodies stuck together and the heat they emitted was overwhelming. If the air conditioning was on, they couldn't tell because it failed to cool them.

For a long time, he kissed her; his lips gripped her's, thick and sticky.

This didn't happen all the time. Not with two kids, Alanie, eight, and Will, six, both of whom happened to be spending the night at a friend's house—a brother and sister of about the same ages, who lived down the street.

Cooling down now, Blaire tried pulling up the covers, but they were too tangled.

"Hold on," Ramsey said. "I need a drink. Want one?"

"Sure, if you're buying," she said.

"After that, it's the least I can do."

"Pretty cheap if you ask me."

Running water sounded from the attached bathroom then stopped.

"You know me," Ramsey said. "I'm into saving a buck. But there was nothing cheap about that."

"No. We need to pawn the kids off on others more often. Let them raise them."

"That could get expensive," Ramsey said, returning with two small paper cups of water.

Slowly, she pulled the covers to a side, exposing a long, white-nyloned leg. "No more expensive than keeping them," she said.

He drank one, then, without thinking, drank the other one.

"Hey!" she said.

"Oh, right."

As Ramsey went for more water, she flung the covers over herself, grabbed the remote, and turned on the TV.

Returning from the bathroom, he sat on the bed and handed her a water.

"What time do you pick them up tomorrow?" he asked.

"Shh!" she said, waving a hand.

A red ribbon with white letters on the bottom of the screen said the news was a Special Report. The sound was turned up and they watched.

2

Saturday morning's light filtered through the sheer curtains into the bedroom. Neither Ramsey nor Blaire had slept a wink. The ongoing coverage on the TV had possessed them.

Need greater than the news, Ramsey had psyched up enough willpower to leave the bed and returned with some coffee.

"Honey," he said, handing her a mug. "What time do you have to pick up the kids?"

"What kids?" she answered.

"Our kids. You birthed them."

"What time is it now?"

"See that little box at the bottom right on the TV. That's the time. Most news channels have them."

"We're okay," she said. "I told them I would pick them up at nine."

"A. M. I presume," Ramsey said. "You know it's nine-o-two, right?"

"Oh, shit!" Blaire threw the covers back, got out of bed for the first time without having to go to the bathroom, opened her closet door, and slipped on some shoes.

"Uh, honey. You may want to get some clothes on."

Blaire looked down at herself. She had never changed out of the white garter and matching nylons.

She grabbed a pair of jeans and slipped them over the stockings. Sneakers went on, then a sweatshirt.

For the first time other than Ramsey going to the bathroom throughout the night and making coffee this morning, she held his attention.

"I guess panties are optional," he said.

"I'll be back," she said, then kissed him goodbye.

"You sure you're okay to drive?"

Apparently, she was. It took longer than usual, but the sound of the garage door going up told Ramsey she had made it. Mom and the two kids walked into a house smelling of french toast, bacon, coffee, and hot chocolate.

"Hey, guys," Ramsey said. "How was it?"

"The usual," Alanie, the eight-year-old said.

Fun!" Will, the six-year-old said, excitement in his voice.

"Come on," their dad said. "Give me a hug."

Will got there first, then Alanie.

"Me, too," their mother said, getting down on one knee in the kitchen.

"We already hugged you," Will said of when she had picked them up.

Needily, she waved her arms for the kids to come to her.

"You know you can hug more than a couple of times a year," Dad said.

Mom's arms wrapped tightly around each child.

"Okay, break it up," Dad said. "Let's eat."

"We already ate," Alanie said. "Janie's mom made us some eggs."

"Eggs *isn't* french toast," Dad said. "Anyone can make eggs. Hell, let's eat up."

Will laughed heartily and finally said when he could breathe again, "You said *hell*."

Dishing out breakfast onto plates, Dad said, "I did say *hell*. And there's plenty of profanity from where that came from, mister."

Will's laugh filled the kitchen. "Like what, Daddy?"

"*Oh*, I don't know. You have one on the tip of your tongue?"

"*Poop!*" the boy blurted.

"Poop?" Dad questioned, handing a plate to Alanie. "That's all you got?"

Will's eyes shifted between his father and his mother.

"I won't get in trouble, will I?" the boy asked.

"How can you?" Dad said. "I'm asking aren't I?"

"Okay, then," the son said. "You asked for it. *Fu…*"

"*William Anderson Keifer!*" Mom interrupted. "You better not finish that word!"

Will's eyes started to tear up. "Dad said I could!"

"And he shouldn't have," Mom countered.

"All I was going to say was…"

"*Will*—don't say it!"

"*Dad?* I have to say it now. I can't leave it on the tip of my tongue."

The boy's tongue appeared out of his mouth and a chubby finger pointed at its tip.

"No, you can't," Ramsey said. "And you shouldn't. Go ahead, buddy, what were you going to say?"

"*Oh, dear Lord,*" Mom mumbled under her breath.

"Fudge!" the boy relieved himself.

"Thank God," Mom said.

"You stain," Alanie said. "Fudge isn't a swear word."

"'*Stain,*'" Dad repeated with raised eyebrows at his wife.

"It is, too," the boy said. "Pappy says it every time he gets mad."

"You smear," the girl began, as both parents looked at each other, shocked, hearing their eight-year-old sound more like a teenager. "He does that around us, so we don't hear the real word—*fu…*"

"Alright," mother interrupted. "Let's eat."

Carrying plates and drinks, they headed for the kitchen table. Bringing up the rear, the parents looked at each other and said, simultaneously, "Pappy," and Blaire went on to say, "and family."

3

Sunday morning came as it had every other week since the day had been named *Sunday* and even before calendars when the day didn't have a name. Ramsey and Blaire sat in the living room, drinking coffee and reading the paper with the news on in the background, just loud enough to hear. Continuing coverage of the Special Report had aired the entire weekend.

Lowering a section of the paper so she could see her husband, she asked, "What are we going to do?"

The section of paper Ramsey had rustled as he lowered it to his lap. "How about a vacation," he suggested.

"A vacation!" she blurted. *"Now?"*

"Sure, why not?"

"Yeah, why not?" said Will, standing in the entranceway.

"Good morning, buddy," Dad said to his son, picking up the remote and turning off the TV.

"Will I miss school?" Will asked.

"I don't know—will you?" Mom asked, grabbing the section of the Sunday paper Ramsey had and rolling it all together with her's and the rest of the newspaper.

"Yeah," the boy said, trotting toward his mother. "If I'm not there."

"That's not what she meant," Alanie said, appearing in the entranceway.

"What about you, squirt?" the father asked his daughter. "Would you like to get out of here and go on a vacation? So far, it's two to one we go."

"Where?" the girl asked.

"Wherever you guys want to go," Dad offered.

"Ramsey," Blaire said. "Don't you think we should have discussed it more?"

"Why discuss it when we're taking it right to a vote?" Ramsey said. "It's more official that way."

"I want to go to Disney World," Will made his desire known.

"Hey," Alanie said. "What if I want to go someplace else?"

"Do you?" Mom asked.

"Sounds like your mom's coming to the good side," Dad said.

"No," the girl said. "Disney's good."

"Three to one, honey," Ramsey said, shrugging his shoulders at his wife.

"Can I bring a friend?" Alanie asked.

"Yeah, me too," Will followed.

"Not on a trip like this," Mom answered. "Parents aren't going to let their kids go on such a long trip without one of them going along."

"Sounds unanimous," Ramsey said.

"But how are we..." Blaire started.

"I know what you're going to ask and I have it all figured out. I'll make some calls tomorrow at work."

Shaking her head, Blaire gave in. "Alright, it's unanimous."

"How about some of those Mickey Mouse pancakes?" Ramsey said.

"*Yay*, pancakes!" Will said, excited.

"I guess," Alanie said, picking up the remote and bouncing on the couch.

"Oh, no you don't," Mom said, standing and taking the remote from her.

"Hey!"

"Come on, let's eat," Mom said, placing the remote and Sunday paper behind a cushion of the chair.

Ramsey knelt before both of his kids, holding each by a forearm.

"Now, listen to me very carefully," he said. "You have to promise me, starting now, there'll be no more TV or radio. If you do, bye-bye Disney. You can put in a disc and watch a movie or play your games. That includes while we're on vacation. We'll come right back here, pronto, if your mom or I catch you. Agreed?"

The kids agreed.

"Don't look so glum," Dad said. "It's only for a couple of weeks."

Blaire's lips pursed, as she looked at her husband, holding back emotion.

While walking into the kitchen together as a family, Will asked, "Dad, what's *you-nanny-mouse* mean?"

4

Nine-thirty and Ramsey just pulled into work. Normally, he reported in a little before eight to get organized and that all-important cup of coffee, but traffic was brutal. To top that off, it was raining.

Parked, he grabbed his stuff and headed for the door. Damn swipe cards in weather like this with one hand holding a briefcase and the other an umbrella made life miserable.

Thoughts like that usually didn't last long once he got inside to his office, thankful the company had invested in security to keep out shooters, disgruntled ex-employees, and the like in this messed up world.

As he stepped inside his office, the inconvenience of the swipe card gave way to familiarity. Briefcase set beside his desk, umbrella left open to dry, and his coat hung, coffee would come first before turning on his computer and getting organized.

Settled at his desk, he checked emails and all the usual.

Ten-fifteen, he picked up his phone and called his broker. During the years Ramsey had worked with him, the guy never answered when he called. Not that he didn't answer because Ramsey had called specifically, more it was his preferred *modus operandi.*

It didn't take long and Ramsey's phone rang.

"Hey, Tom," Ramsey answered. "Thanks for getting back to me so soon."

"Of course," Tom said. "I would have gotten back sooner, but my phone's been ringing off the hook and I should have a revolving door installed in my office. Enough of my problems, what can I help you with?"

"Sell everything, would you?"

"Probably a good idea to take what gain you have left. The market's down sharply this morning based on the news. I'm entering the trades now. It might take a little longer to sell than usual because there aren't many buyers, but don't worry, someone will."

"I know you'll do your best. And hey, Tom. Once they sell, could you have the money sent to my bank account."

"After they settle, sure thing. It'll take a couple of days."

"That's fine," Ramsey said.

"You guys getting out of dodge?" Tom asked.

"Yeah."

"Where are you guys going?"

"Disney."

"*Oh, yeah.* Land or World?"

"World. It's closer."

"I hear Land's better, but World's nice. Kids will like it."

"I hope so," Ramsey said.

"A couple of these went already," Tom said.

"Great. I knew you were good."

"*Ah,* damn phone again. But all of your orders are placed. You should see the money in your bank account three days or so from now if they all sell today. I have to ask. I know you said all of it, but did you want to leave some in the account?"

"No. I was going to close it."

"I totally get it. I'll close it once everything settles and the transfer is made. There might be straggling dividends and things like that."

"Keep them for all I care. I'm not worried about it."

"Okay. Better see who called. Take care, Ramsey."

"You, too, Tom."

Ramsey hung up the phone and stared at it.

Michael, a co-worker, stepped into the office. "How's it going, Ram?"

"Okay, I guess. You?"

"The same. Today your last day?"

"Yeah. Your's, too, right?"

Michael looked around Ramsey's office, then said, "Yep. Today's the day."

Seeing the box in Michael's hand, Ramsey asked, "Packing it in?"

"Just finished. I didn't see the point in doing any work. Here's an extra box if you would like one." Michael set it on the floor.

"Printer paper box. I was on my way there next."

"Don't bother. I swiped this one before they all disappeared."

"I think a box will do, thanks."

"They're having cake in the break room around lunch if you want to grab a piece."

"Sure."

Michael's eyes roamed the office again as he said, "I'm sure going to miss our talks."

"Me, too," Ramsey said.

"Who's going to get the promotion, office politics, the latest gossip, warning each other to avoid the bathroom because someone gassed it up, and guessing who the culprit was just doesn't matter anymore does it?"

"No. I guess not. A complete waste of time."

"Yeah, but we had a good time talking about it."

"It sure did pass the time."

Michael's hand slapped the door frame and he said, "Well, I'll stop down around noon and we'll grab some cake. One last hurrah before we leave this joint."

"Sounds good," Ramsey said. "And Michael—thanks for

the box."

Around two-fifteen, Ramsey pulled into his garage. Blaire opened the garage door to meet him and to help carry anything in.

"How did it go?" she asked.

"About as good as it could, I guess," Ramsey said. "How about you? All packed up?"

"Almost."

"That's good. And, *oh*, I called Tom and he's selling everything. The money should be in the bank account in three or four days if we're lucky."

"Three or four days? What do we do until then?"

"We don't need it, honey. Not yet, anyway. There's plenty in savings to get us by for a bit."

He carried the box inside the house and she brought in some smaller items. They set everything on the kitchen floor and she hugged him.

"I know you liked that job, dear," she said. "I'm so sorry."

"Don't be," he said and kissed her. "Things are what they are."

Her twinkling eyes took in her husband. His strength with this made her proud. Usually, he would have blown up at a time like this, but circumstances were different. The company hadn't asked him to leave—he walked away. It wasn't any less scary, but the difference between the two was huge.

"*Oh*, and I booked everything for Disney," Ramsey said. "That's why I stayed at work."

"And for *goodbyes* I'm sure," she said.

"A couple of people stopped by."

"Well … they can have it. Old habits die hard. I'm glad you're not like that."

"You'll think differently of me in a few hours from now. Traveling is going to be a royal pain in the ass. But, you're right, for many of those jokesters, the habit will never die. I think too much of myself to let a habit rule my universe."

"And that's why you rule mine," she said and kissed him.

5

Traveling *was* a royal pain in the ass. Literally. Already, the family grew irritable and tired of sitting. The twenty-mile, forty-minute drive to Baltimore-Washington International Airport ended up taking nearly two hours. Ramsey had expected clogged highways, but that was obscene.

A CD in the disc player passed the time.

Parking could be only described as vile. There weren't any spots, so Ramsey had created his own. Finally, the CD on its fifth consecutive play turned off when Ramsey stopped it. The radio on, a reporter said mid-sentence, "…is truly and utterly remarkable," a pause, then, "You've been listening to uninterrupted, live coverage of this special broadcast…"

Ramsey turned it off and, with his fingers still on the knob, looked at Blaire.

"Sorry about that," Ramsey said as he turned off the car. "But Disney will be worth it. I promise."

The human traffic outside and inside the airport grossed the family out. They had been to sporting events, amusement parks, and such where there had been many people, one hundred thousand, fifty thousand, confined to one area. But when there's no place to maneuver, gridlocked, waiting too long for hallways, staircases, and escalators to clear out, it caused the patient to become impatient, the polite unpolite, and the un-claustrophobic to now suffer from the disease.

Ramsey and Blaire diffused as much of the chaos as they could by ensuring the kids, "They're in a hurry, that's all," "They're trying to make their flight," "Or catch a cab," "Or get home."

TV screens were all over the place, displaying the most up-to-date weather at nearly every major city in the United States and abroad where flights were heading, flight schedules, and—continuing coverage of the Special Report.

When the Keifers had arrived at their gate, seats and the floor of the waiting area wasn't visible, buried beneath a layer of humanity.

There's too many, Ramsey thought. *Too many to fit on the plane.*

Maybe they were waiting for family or friends on an incoming plane. He sure hoped so.

It had taken so long to get to this point, that it shouldn't be long now before they parked the plane and began boarding.

So, the family stood and waited. While facing the seating area and gate, Blaire saw a picture on one of the TVs and tapped Ramsey. Ramsey followed her eyes and couldn't help but stare himself.

Breaking out of the trance, he bent over and said to the kids, "We're going to face this way, okay. Stare at this wall for a little bit. Anyone feeling claustrophobic? I am. So let's stare at these nice people along the wall instead of all of them out there."

The family turned around together.

"You know what," he continued. "Why don't you guys sit on our feet. Remember doing that?"

The kids sat on the tops of their parent's shoes.

"That's it," Mom said.

"Yeah, snuggle in there and get nice and comfortable," Dad said.

Sitting in his seat on the taxiing plane, Ramsey wasn't even close to his family. A last-minute booking, only a few scattered seats had remained in coach on the near-capacity plane. Ramsey sat alone near the back, Blaire alone near the front, and the two kids together near the middle—not over the wing. The wing seats had already been reserved, so Ramsey knew there wouldn't be an issue with where the kids sat.

Ramsey had given Alanie his cell phone and set it to text messaging so Blaire could check up on them now and again.

Divided like that, of course, the parents hated it, but what choice did they have? None, if they wanted to get to Disney.

With flying specifically into Orlando, Florida, crowded flights and altered routes had limited Ramsey's choices when he had booked the flights. The fact that he could get four seats on the same flight let alone two together for the kids made him feel fortunate.

That was then; this is now. A five-and-a-half hour, two-stop flight awaited them.

Landing at Orlando International Airport, Blaire exited the plane first, then the kids, then Ramsey, who tried to plead his case to move up with his children, but only got so far from a few nice folks, who had let him go ahead of them.

Ignoring complaining passengers, telling her to move, Blaire waited for the kids in the passenger boarding bridge. There was no way she was going to proceed to the terminal and wait for them there among the sea of people, funneling out of the gangway. Besides, if Orlando's seating area near the gate was anything like Baltimore's, her babies could be kidnapped, trampled, or worse.

Pushing through people to get to them, Blaire turned the tide, telling people to move and let her kids through. Once she had them, she hugged them and they proceeded through the bridge to the terminal.

Eventually, Ramsey appeared out of the bridge and Blaire and the kids waved to him.

He made his way to his family and loathed the idea of having to fetch their bags at the baggage claim. Getting there would undoubtedly be the pits and he had already decided that he would be the one to fight through the crowd to grab the bags, while Blaire held both kids in her arms, someplace in the background, to avoid all of that mess.

And that's how it went.

Having their bags and each other, the Keifers still had to take the monorail from the terminal to the main airport building. They did, under crowded and unpleasant conditions.

Now, from the main airport building, Ramsey and his family had to get to the resort. So far, everything had been unavoidable. But now was Ramsey's time to shine. While researching and planning the trip, he had stumbled upon a way of avoiding the highways, byways, Greenways, Parkways, and Interstates.

Typically, it would have taken only a half-an-hour to drive the twenty-five miles between the Orlando Airport to Disney's Grand Floridian Resort & Spa. Not bad. Driving would have been a viable option.

Not now. The estimated drive time had quadrupled, no matter which way they chose. The Expressway to Interstate 4 and over. The Greenway and over. Even heading farther south on Access Road to the Parkway and over. Royalty pain would have graduated to deity pain.

So, to avoid all of that mess, Ramsey had arranged a surprise. After he and his family found the security office, someone there escorted them to the roof.

"Whoa!" Will blurted out. "Are we riding on that?"

"We sure are, buddy," Dad said.

Skepticism flushed Blaire's face white.

A helicopter sat on a helipad.

"It'll be alright," Ramsey said, looking into her eyes and nodding reassuringly. "What's the difference? In a car with all of those mad people out there, or in that thing—or something else."

Color returned to her face as she got his point. "You're right," she said.

"You're in good hands, ma'am," the security guard said. "For years this guy's been making runs for the bank right below the H of this pad. Not once had anything bad happened."

While walking up to Ramsey, the pilot had heard the guard and said as he shook Ramsey's hand, "Way to jinx us." He took the bag from Blaire and said, "Let's go. I want to get home myself."

"You heard him," Ramsey said.

The pilot had gone above and beyond, flying the family over every major Disney property complete with the typical spiel he had said so many times during aerial tours that his words were for informational purposes only, lacking any enthusiasm whatsoever.

Epcot's silver ball got the most reaction out of Will, while the castle at the Magic Kingdom stirred excitement in Alanie.

For over an hour, they flew around and the pilot turned to Ramsey and asked, "Is that good?"

The kids' beaming faces gave Ramsey his answer.

"You bet," Ramsey said. "We loved it."

"Well, good," the pilot said. "Glad I could be of service."

The helicopter flew over Grand Floridian Resort & Spa a couple of times and then descended toward one of the nearby parking lots that had now become a helipad because there was a considerable H painted on the blacktop.

The pilot landed the craft and shut it down. When the blades stopped spinning, the pilot unbuckled the kids out of their seats and helped them down out of the chopper.

The family moved to a safe distance, while Ramsey

remained by the helicopter with an upright suitcase beside him. He handed the pilot a wad of cash. After counting it, the pilot, selectively, pulled out a couple of bills and handed them back to Ramsey. They said their goodbyes and the pilot climbed back inside the chopper, while Ramsey picked up the suitcase and headed toward his family.

Blaire thought her husband looked like a soldier returning home from Vietnam, carrying his seabag with the helicopter behind him.

As the chopper's blades spun, picking up speed, Blaire yelled to her husband, "What's the damage?"

"Damaging," Ramsey said. "You don't want to know."

"Give me a ballpark."

"Ten times what that tour normally costs. But, he gave some back."

"I saw. So, we're still afloat?"

"Yeah, we're okay. It was a small iceberg. We won't sink."

6

Despite the ass pain in getting to Disney, the helicopter ride and aerial tour had soothed it over like a miracle ointment.

Their room at the resort also contained healing properties, and, magically in the magic kingdom, caused selective amnesia, because the helicopter was the only part of the trip anyone talked about or remembered.

One of the things Ramsey remembered was how less occupied the Disney properties were, specifically, within the boundaries of Interstate 4, the Floride Turnpike, and the Beltway.

Now, there were other people there, of course. It wasn't as if the Keifers had the resort and attractions all to themselves. Others had the same idea.

Starting with the helicopter ride, Disney was panning out to be a fabulous trip. Breakfasts with characters (even Will liked the princesses), the character parades, the shows, rides—everything. They park-hopped to every park and the nice thing was none of them were packed. In fact, quite empty for this time of year. The kids got to ride the rides many times over, getting off and right back on.

The parents considered renting a car and venturing

outside the park area on their own to do some things, especially with the Disney area contained as it was, but decided against it. Let the shuttle vans and buses chauffeur them around.

They stayed at arguably Disney's best resort, the Grand Floridian Resort & Spa, and ate at all of the best places—damn the costs—and that the kids would like, of course. Except for one of the best restaurants, conveniently located at the resort, but inconveniently and quite unacceptable, no children under the age of ten were allowed admittance.

The kids probably wouldn't have liked it anyway.

A grille perched atop Disney's Contemporary Resort had crossed their minds to catch a panoramic view of a special pyrotechnics show where fireworks would be coordinatingly launched from every Disney theme park. Disney claimed it would be the best show of its kind ever in all of human history and would break nearly every pyrotechnic achievement found in the Guinness Book of World Records.

In their room at the resort, Ramsey asked the kids, "You guys hungry?"

"*Na*, not really," Will said.

"Me neither," Alanie said.

"We have eaten like pigs, haven't we," Dad said, then asked his wife, "Honey, what about you?"

"I'm not starving, but I could eat something," Blaire answered.

"We all know what that means, don't we kids," Dad said, as he reached out and tickled Alanie, nearby, and then Will when he ran up to be tickled, too.

"She's hungry," Dad and his two kids said almost simultaneously; the kids through nearly out-of-breath squeals from being tickled.

Everyone caught their breath and then Dad said, "Maybe if we tickle your mom's belly she won't be hungry."

As Ramsey and the two kids approached their mom—the kids with their hands raised like zombies—Mom said, "Or become hungrier," then she growled as her family went into full tickle-attack mode.

Mom fell on top of one of the beds and the family piled on. The kids were in top form tonight, tickling in all of the right areas their mother found ticklish. Ramsey backed off and tickles turned into kisses on her laughing red face.

The moment died down and the family un-piled off her like defensive players getting to their feet after making a tackle in a football game.

"You guys think of what kind of food you want to eat," Ramsey said, "while I go talk to the concierge to see what they recommend."

"Alright, Dad," Will said, being a good sport.

Ramsey grabbed Blaire's hands and pulled, helping her off the bed. Their bodies collided and he whispered in her ear, "I'm going to see what's going on."

They looked at each other and all she could do was nod, holding back emotion.

"Okay," Ramsey said, breaking the tension. "I'll be back in two minutes and we're off."

Ramsey hadn't lied, he did stop briefly at the concierge desk to see what restaurants they recommended. Most, they had already eaten at, so it wasn't a help. Which, is what he figured.

He stepped into a lounge, surprised to see it empty. There was a TV attached to the wall holding the liquor behind the bar.

"Television again, sir?" the bartender asked Ramsey.

This wasn't the first time Ramsey had stopped in. Sometimes for an occasional drink, but every time to catch the news. Specifically, the Special Report he couldn't help noticing everywhere he went.

"Yes," Ramsey said. "I'm afraid so."

A grimace contorted the bartender's face.

Ramsey thought the bartender would make a good butler. It wouldn't have surprised him if he had been one once. His appearance, mannerisms, and accent stereotyped the man into the role.

Waving a finger and sitting on a barstool, Ramsey said, "I'll have a Cognac. Hennessy XO. Neat."

"Looks like we'll make our numbers for the night," the bartender said, sarcastically.

He had that going for him, too, in making him the ideal butler.

The bartender grabbed the Hennessy bottle by the neck as if lifting a dumbbell, displayed its label to Ramsey, tapped a finger on the X.O., pulled the cork out, and poured some into a snifter. His eyes rolled up to look at Ramsey and then he poured some more. Then, some more.

"That's generous," Ramsey said. "Thank you."

Another pour filled the snifter just below the rim. The bottle was corked and put away; then the bartender set the snifter on the marble bar in front of Ramsey.

"Mind if I join you?" the bartender asked, lifting an already-poured sifter out from under the bar that he must have been sipping prior to Ramsey's arrival. He turned the volume up on the TV.

7

Back in the room, the kids were bored.

"Can we watch TV until Dad gets back?" Will asked his mother.

"No!" she answered. "No TV."

"But I'm bored."

"Do you want to break your promise to your dad?"

"No," Will pouted.

"Okay then."

"Do you want to play a card game?" Alanie asked her brother.

Mom wiped a tear from her eye. "That's a good girl, Alanie."

"I guess," Will answered, disgusted. "Nothing else to do."

In the lounge, Ramsey worked on drinking the generous pour of cognac in his sifter, which wasn't small in its own right. In a crunch, the bowled glass could house a number of goldfish comfortably as would any fishbowl.

He and the bartender watched the Special Report. The images broadcasted were beyond belief. And hard to turn away from. Perhaps, subconsciously, when he had the kids promise not to watch TV or listen to the radio, he should have promised himself.

No loving parent would do that. Information had to be obtained for proper parenting.

Five, simple words, everyday words, but usually not arranged to make the phrase bannered at the bottom of the TV screen, told him everything he needed to know. And knowing made it easier for him to consume his drink much faster than he usually would have.

"I'm sure you're not driving," the bartender said, "taxiing the fam in Disney's finest style. So, would you like another? The lounge will be closing soon."

"I better not," Ramsey answered. "*Whew!* I'm going to have a good buzz going."

"It's the best way to enjoy the festivities. Sure I can't tempt you to stay?" The bartender picked up the bottle by the neck, doing exactly what he had said—tempting Ramsey. "I don't have any plans this evening."

"You should do something."

"I thought about watching the show from the top of the Contemporary Resort. I think I'll take this bottle with me. The drive will set the right mood for drinking the whole thing."

"We were looking at that place, too, to watch the fireworks. Looks like it will be a great view. Better leave now, though, or you'll miss the beginning."

"We wouldn't want that, would we?"

Ramsey stood out of the stool, knowing he should get back to his family. "Thanks again for the use of the TV."

"Don't thank me," the bartender said. "It's not mine. Besides, it's included in your room bill."

"It'll be a pain, but I hope you go over there. Either way, enjoy the show—and take care."

"You and your family do the same."

They waved to each other and Ramsey headed back to the room.

Blaire paced the room, unaware she was doing it, while the kids played a card game. Earlier, she had tried reaching Ramsey by texting his cell phone, but it buzzed on the nightstand in the room.

The door clicked and Ramsey entered.

"Where were you?" Blaire blurted, then lowered her voice. "It's been almost half-an-hour."

"I know. I know," Ramsey started. "Listen…"

"You had a drink?" she interrupted. "I don't care, but…"

"What did you have, Dad?" Will interjected. "A Coke?"

"Yeah, buddy," Dad said. "A Coke is all."

"It's so damn…" she whispered.

"I know," he said. "Don't say it. Listen."

"What's happening?"

"Two hours," he whispered in her ear.

That stopped her cold. Distant, lost eyes pointed at her husband, but they weren't looking—not really.

"Less now, honey," he said. "If we're going to go, let's go. I want to. I mean, there are lots of worse places…"

"I know." His wife had returned. "We should go."

"Okay," he said, then he asked the kids, "so you guys decide what you want to eat?"

"I didn't think about it," Alanie admitted.

"Me neither," Will said.

"Well, what were you guys doing besides playing cards?" Dad asked.

"Waiting for you," Alanie answered.

That brought a chuckle to both Dad and Mom.

"What do you want, hon?" Ramsey asked his wife. "You were the one who was hungry."

"Hell, let's live a little," Blaire said. "How about ice cream?"

"Yeah, ice cream!" Will blurted.

Alanie's head nodded on her neck and her tongue licked her lips she agreed.

"Ice cream it is!" Dad said. "But we better get going."

8

They ended up at the Magic Kingdom to grab some ice cream and watch the fireworks.

It was becoming harder for Ramsey and Blaire to distract the kids, pointing here and there and saying, "Look at that," "Check that out," "There's Mickey,"—as the mouse ran by.

People screaming didn't help. Neither did them rushing for the gates, occasionally looking back over their shoulder. Sounds, normally not heard at Disney, had to sound wrong to the kids, even though they had never been there before or knew any better.

Blaire covered Alanie's ears with her hands, Ramsey's over Will's, as they ushered them inside the ice cream parlor. Inside, they relaxed a little.

Pastel colors made the place a little girly, Will thought, but he had been to other amusements to know those types of colors were usually representative of cotton candy, candy, and ice cream.

A man wearing a Coppola hat, striped shirt, and apron asked, "What'll be?"

As the family reviewed the menu board over the counter, the man continued, "Did you see the sign outside?"

"No, we didn't," Ramsey answered.

"Whatever you choose, it's all you can eat. So choose wisely."

Utter surprise elongated both Ramsey and Blaire's faces as they looked at each other.

"Okay, no pressure then," Ramsey said a little offbeat. "Kids, you don't want to get stuck eating something you don't like."

"Or, if you don't like it, don't eat it," the ice cream man said. "Wasting a few bucks isn't going to matter."

"Right," Ramsey said. Things must be getting to him—or the cognac.

The family decided and ordered. There wasn't a rush because there was only an old couple waiting to order behind them. Behind the counter, a team of two, probably man and wife, the owners of the place, went to work.

Ramsey paid and they all went outside to sit.

Few tables were occupied, so Blaire chose where she thought they could see the fireworks best.

They sat down under an umbrella, which blocked the night sky on Main Street, U.S.A.

The kid's ice cream held their attention through the first bite and then...

"Whoa!" A surprised Will said, pointing toward Cinderella's Castle. "What's that?"

9

Just then, fireworks launched into the night sky behind the iconic castle.

"It's all part of the show," Dad said. "Remember Universal Studios? How life-like everything was?"

"Yeah," Will said.

"Like that."

The entire trip, up to that moment, the kids had been so distracted and having fun that they seldom looked up at the sky—or at least in the direction to see something. Why should they with so much to see and do down here on the ground?

Purposefully, the parents had mapped out what parks they wanted to hit and when—and why. Every Disney park contained outside attractions, rides, and eateries, so the parents had them cruise through the more outdoorsy parks earlier in the trip and progressively wean to the least outdoorsy ones nearing the end.

Until tonight.

"But, what is it?" Alanie asked.

Until tonight.

"Yeah, Dad, what is it?" Will mimicked.

Until tonight.

Emotion erupted out of Blaire like a volcano relieving itself, forceful and powerful from her holding it in.

Until tonight, when it didn't matter. There was no use in protecting the kids anymore when there wasn't a way to protect them. Nowhere to go to protect them. Nothing they could do to change the circumstances and save them. Their tickets to Disney World had been one way. Exorbitant costs had become easy to pay because there was no future to save for. The last week was all the retirement they would get. There'll be no college. No weddings. No grandkids. No more birthday parties. Vacations. Meals. Nothing. Not even life.

Will's inquisitive mind thought about the movies, shows, and cartoons he had watched and the video games he had just started learning to play and he offered, "It looks like a world."

10

T h e five, simple words Ramsey and the bartender had read on the TV screen in the lounge were, "Impact expected within two hours."

That was over an hour ago.

Ramsey's arm wrapped around his boy and his hand squeezed his shoulder. "That's my boy," the proud father said.

"Such a smart boy," Blaire said through tears, reaching a hand out to hold her son's hand. "And girl," she added, hugging Alanie, who cried, only because her mother was crying.

"Why is it here?" the boy asked. "Is it aliens?"

"Oh my God, Ramsey!" Mom blurted. "I can't take this."

As Ramsey stood out of his chair, he grabbed Will's shirt for him to stand and move out from the table. Connected from years of marriage, Blaire stood when her husband had and brought Alanie with her. They hugged there, outside the ice cream parlor on Main Street, U.S.A. of Disney's Magic Kingdom, with the pointed turrets of Cinderella's Castle behind them, a fireworks display worthy of the record books above the castle, and a pale-yellow surface of a unknown world behind it all, reflecting the Sun's light, and so close now, when Will peeked, he felt like he could reach up and touch it.

Many in the park panicked, doing things they typically wouldn't have done. Killing their loved ones before the oncoming world could. Killing themselves, not giving the world the satisfaction. For these people, nothing could distract them from the pending doom.

Others derived as much pleasure as they could out of the time they had left. Some were glad, feeling the world deserved such a fate.

A number of people dropped dead—the whole experience too much to take and carry on, even for a few moments more.

The old couple, who had been in line to order ice cream behind Ramsey and his family, pondered their life and patiently waited. They were of an age where death had been standing outside the door, even knocked a few times, but hadn't opened it yet.

A few at the ice cream parlor and even fewer passing by saw Ramsey and his family and figured hugging whoever they came to the park with was the right thing to do and did it themselves.

Now well into the eleventh hour, minutes until midnight, Ramsey, age thirty-four, Blaire, age thirty-two, Alanie, age eight, and Will, age six, held each other tight and waited for the end of the world.

11

From what Ramsey had seen on the TV back at the resort, death would come quick. Earth wouldn't withstand the collision with the oncoming world larger than Jupiter. Everything scientists and speculators had theorized about what would happen in a scenario such as this hadn't been wrong, but in this instance, although it didn't look like it in the sky, the world raced toward Earth at such a high speed, that all of its forces imposed on the Earth's moon, atmosphere, and Earth itself, would be brief before collision. It's gravitational pull on the moon and Earth intensified and who knew what other planets and celestial bodies this gigantic orb had brought with it during its travels. Inevitably, some sections of the Earth would rise into formations, others would sink, creating recesses, and then there would be parts that remained where they have always been. Volcanoes. Fissures opening. Earth stressed like no other time in its history except, perhaps, its formation. Displaced water. Rolling, ever-climbing tides. All of which and things unfathomed would take place simultaneously in the briefest of time.

Perhaps the brevity with which the Earth would be destroyed signified a mercy gesture. Ramsey and his wife didn't feel that way. Why couldn't this have happened a million years from now? Or even a million years before? Why did *they* have to experience it?

And experience it, they did. The clock struck midnight. The assaulting world was so close now that it had lost its circular shape and dominated the sky. It was as if space had become bored with black and changed color to a pale-yellow. The sun, reflecting off the world, had turned nighttime into day. The best display of fireworks in human history continued, because Ramsey could hear them, but could no longer see them, lost in the world's illumination.

The Earth rumbled under their feet and Ramsey and his family couldn't hear the exploding fireworks anymore.

"Close your eyes," Ramsey said to his family. "Don't watch it."

They held each other tighter than they ever had to anything. Alanie cried. Will cried. Blaire cried. Ramsey cried—and peeked.

Simultaneously, rods of earth spiked through buildings—and people—on Main Street, U.S.A., while other structures and people disappeared into swallowing mouths of Earth.

Things were tossed about. Large things, like buildings, vehicles, and rides with humans still in them.

More and more debris ascended toward the mauling world. So much so that in no time, the debris, racing into the sky toward it, scratched across the world's surface.

This was it—the world was ending.

Ramsey kissed Alanie, then Will, and lastly Blaire. They had experienced so much together—including the end of the world and, likely soon, their death.

Water from the Gulf of Mexico had engulfed the western half of Florida and the Atlantic Ocean the entire east side. Both displaced bodies of water were converging on central Florida—on Disney.

Then, introduced within the sounds of unraveling Earth, Ramsey heard a loud—what? There was no way of describing, accurately, all of the sights and sounds happening around him and his family. No one living had ever experienced such annihilation before and there was no way of escaping it.

Anything could kill them. Flying debris. Being sucked into the air. Swallowed by the Earth. Drowning in the approaching waters.

"I love you guys!" Ramsey yelled to his family. "Alanie. Will. Blaire, the love of my life and soon eternity. Take my love with you and I'll remember yours. Know you were loved."

If they had responded, he couldn't hear them. He hoped they had heard him.

Something wet sprinkled Ramsey's face. With arms and hands pressing his family's faces into his body, he yelled, "Don't look!"

Experiencing the loudest, constant sounds they ever heard, he doubted anyone had heard him.

A cold liquid washed over their sneakers and sandals and, immediately after, a wave of cold liquid rolled forcefully against their shins. At this point, it could be anything.

Holding his family tight against him, Ramsey first looked down, then up and around as far as his neck could go. Two towering, black walls of ocean water raced toward each other—toward Disney—closing in on the Keifers.

As the bodies of water drew close, gusting wind intensified, racing through the water corridor, powerful enough to lift the children's feet off the ground and the adult's flirting with occasional separation.

"Don't look!" Ramsey yelled to his family. "Please! Don't let this be the last images you see!"

Not heeding his own words, Ramsey watched the sky-high bodies of water, taller than any skyscraper, close-in. Closer now, there were things in the water that shouldn't be.

Strangely, he wondered if this was what it had been like like for the Hebrews when they passed through the parted Red Sea; the pale-yellow world peering down at him through the hall of water the Pharoah of Egypt himself in hot pursuit.

No, at this moment, Ramsey didn't find anything merciful about a quick death. Humans are powerless against death, no matter how it happens or the timing. Waiting to die, he felt that now—powerless—as the water reached the height of his children, swooshing their hair and quickly rising.

Knowing it was impossible for his family to hear, he yelled anyway, "I love you guys! Oh, how I love you!"

All eight feet of the Keifer family rose off the ground as the two oceans, carrying many a man and his remnants, headed for a collision—a collision the Keifers would not survive.

Still, Ramsey hoped their deaths would be quick and painless.

FOREWORD

A publisher emailed me with information about a writing contest in case I was interested and wanted to submit. I've never entered a writing contest before and, after looking over the information, I felt I should try it.

There were all sorts of guidelines to follow. The story had to be fifty paragraphs long with the first and twenty-fifth paragraphs already written and provided—bolded in the story for differentiation—leaving forty-eight paragraphs to the writer's imagination. There were other rules, but who cares.

A Fatal Thing found life in my head. When I finished recording it, my wife and I read it and liked it, so I submitted the story.

I didn't win the contest.

A Fatal Thing

Beyond the cracked sidewalk, and the telephone pole with layers of flyers in a rainbow of colors, and the patch of dry brown grass there stood a ten-foot high concrete block wall, caked with dozens of coats of paint. There was a small shrine at the foot of it, with burnt out candles and dead flowers and a few soggy teddy bears. One word of graffiti filled the wall, red letters on a gold background: Rejoice!

There were similar memorials like it all over the world. Headstones, really. All different sizes and shapes, remembering the dead and honoring heroes, who had sacrificed themselves to preserve human existence. But none like this one. Although small and crude, this shrine fit the definition, because the man enshrined here in Uganda's

Capital City, Kampala had sacrificed himself so others may live.

Doctor Park Gombya, a respected Molecular Virologist, had spent two weeks in Liberia, Africa, working with other scientists on another Ebola breakout in that area. During the last leg of a twelve-hour flight home, the question of whether humans were alone in the universe had been answered emphatically.

As he looked out his seat window, a massive, bright star appeared, seemingly, out of nowhere in the distant sky. Its brilliance during daytime hours seemed highly unusual. At first, it was hard to tell whether the light was artificial or natural. Then it moved farther into the distance at a speed that made it seem to disappear. Nothing appeared in the sky like that again for the rest of the flight.

As Doctor Gombya's plane descended for landing at Entebbe International Airport, a brilliant light hovered over Uganda's Capital City, Kampala, twenty-seven miles north of the airport. It wasn't until he was on the ground, under it, that Doctor Gombya could make out what it was.

The twenty-seven-mile drive home usually took about an hour. But with every driver preoccupied with the lighted square in the sky, it had taken a lot longer. Approaching the city of Kampala, where the Doctor lived, he had been right on the plane—the light in the daytime sky was hovering over the capital city.

To his surprise, a silvery beam of light flashed out of the bottom of the peculiar square and touched Earth. From what Doctor Gombya could tell, nothing had been damaged. Then another beam. And another. Until, many beams emitted from the craft, simultaneously; the whole thing resembled a wrongly-shaped disco ball.

Challenging nearly every understanding of aerodynamics, the hovering craft moved left with a corner of the square as its front, while more silver beams touched Earth now at a greater distance. The opposite corner moved it right and so on until the flat, squared ship continuously moved like a joystick—front, back, and side-to-side—while laser beams ceaselessly connected the ship with Earth. Yet, there was no damage, from what Doctor Gombya could tell. The spaceship's light show ended and once more it hovered, stationary, over the capital city.

Then, he saw one—a creature from the ship—on the ground—an alien. Heaven's sake, it was awful. Not of this world nor resembled anything how humans have depicted celestial beings for millennia. Nevertheless, this creature came from the heavens—meaning from somewhere in space.

It had a Ugandan woman's head in its mouth, struggling with it as humans do with dangerously large hard candy. How its mouth enlarged wide enough to swallow a human head whole confused the Doctor. Disorientation had him driving right for what he didn't understand. When he veered enough to miss them, the alien had the headless corpse raised in defense and, in doing so, must have squeezed the body or cracked the head in its mouth because blood splattered on the passenger side window of the vehicle as he drove by.

In his rearview mirror, the alien continued to hold up the corpse with what the Doctor could only describe as *clingers*, claws with fingers, as more aliens converged on the human flesh for their share. The woman's body disappeared in a gang of aliens. Their aggressive behavior communicated what he couldn't see—nor wanted to see.

A terrified Doctor Gombya had to slam on the brakes to avoid smashing into standstill traffic ahead. The tires squealed and eventually skidded the car to a stop. Two miles of bumper-to-bumper traffic lined the road between him and the city. The ease with which the alien creatures were smashing into vehicles and consuming the occupants screamed to the shocked Doctor that it wasn't safe for him to stay in the car. In his state, home was the only place that came to mind to go. He grabbed his briefcase and left everything else behind for the city.

Gruesome murders occurred all around him. Not only were humans not alone in the universe, but these creatures were hostile. They came to feed on mankind and only time would tell if they had other motives for coming to Earth and how long they would stay. If what he witnessed here was happening all over the world, no human would be left to see if the creatures had alternative motives or not, because humans would be extinct.

Adrenaline, motivated by self-preservation and, perhaps, the preservation of humankind, spirited elusive dodging by the Doctor in avoiding the aliens on the ground as he used to do in games of tag on this very land when he was a boy.

A mile closer to home, the fearful Doctor stumbled upon the university where he worked. *Did I bring the keys*, he thought and checked his pocket. He had. His trembling hands fumbled with the keys and, before he could identify the key to open the office building door, they fell to the ground.

As he bent over to pick them up, something grabbed his arm. A *clinger*—one of those claws with fingers. In pulling his arm out with keys in hand, what could only be described as sharp fingernails, sliced deep wounds on both sides of his forearm below the elbow. Only in a short-sleeved shirt, nothing hindered the surgical incisions.

The Doctor ran for the building, unsure if he could unlock it and, even if he did, would the glass doors be enough to keep the alien creature from entering. If metal and glass in automobiles weren't strong enough to keep aliens out, the glass doors in the building surely wouldn't keep them out either.

The alien pursued. Just when the Doctor didn't think he was going to make it inside, a garbage truck plowed into the extraterrestrial, pushing him a distance away until the celestial body slithered down the front of the truck and under its wheels. Tearing his eyes away, Doctor Gombya unlocked the door and proceeded to his office.

From his office window, he witnessed things he wished

he never had. His adult life had been spent examining Ebola and containing its breakouts to an unlucky few. Now, a more immediate danger had come to Earth, threatening everyone. Earth, its creatures, and its inhabitants already produce lethal killers. The last thing the world needed was something else to contend with. And contend some did. *Thank goodness for the driver of the garbage truck*, he thought.

Then and there, looking out his office window, Doctor Park Gombya decided to compete, too. The way to do it came to him as clear as anything ever had in his entire life. Maybe he had been born for just a time as this.

His own thoughts betrayed him. *Born for what? To be eaten?* Courage gave way to second thoughts, spurred on by remembering how an alien had taken the Ugandan woman's head in its stretched mouth and torn it off her body.

Remaining at the office or doing what he had felt so compelled to do earlier would betray his family. He should be home with them, protecting them as a good father should. Why should he shoulder the weight of the world?

The world weighed too much. A dilemma on top of everything happening wasn't fair. Forcing the Doctor to choose between his family and trying something that might not work muddied the waters. There was no reason he shouldn't go to his family. It was the rational thing to do.

Or was it? Was fighting back his calling? Above all else, a husband, father, and all those two words mean, contending with the aliens was a higher calling. No different than the driver using a garbage truck to fight; a truck in which the driver had probably driven nearly every day.

Moments later, Doctor Gombya left the campus building and walked boldly toward center city Kampala, the Capital City of Uganda—his home. Amazingly, as if protected by a force greater than himself, he walked nearly a mile, untouched. So close now to center city, he ran like a sprinter for the finish line. Out of energy and breath, he stopped. A blood-stained creature seized him, slammed his body against a concrete block wall, and swallowed his whiplashed head.

Other aliens saw the capture and greedily gathered around his body. Collectively, they devoured Doctor Park Gombya, bones and all.

Three days later an automobile pulled up and parked beside the concrete wall. The driver opened the door, but did not get out of the car. Although her face was in shadow, it was easy to tell she was sad. There was something about how she turned away from the sun and rested the weight of her hands on the steering wheel, something about her silent composure that caused Hannah to sigh. The young girl watched the driver lean out of the car and stretch her hand out towards one of the burned out candles.

Hannah, a homeless teen, who had nowhere to go and no one to be with the day the aliens invaded, had hidden inside a dumpster in an unpaved alley of dry, brown grass and dead spots of dirt between the bank and the courthouse. The dumpster and smell of it had probably saved her life.

From it, she had witnessed Doctor Gombya's death, not knowing who he was or what he had done. It had scared her enough to remain in the dumpster for three days, eating what she could from the waste and when it had rained, she reached a tin can out from under the lid and drank what it had collected.

Now, only a ten-foot-high concrete block section of wall was all that remained of the courthouse; the rest had been destroyed during the war with the aliens. This wall was where Doctor Park Gombya had been killed and consumed, so it had become a shrine, dedicated to his memory and what he had started. Painted before the rain came, the gold courthouse wall had come to represent his heart of gold, still standing in judgment against the aliens and the word *Rejoice!*, painted in red, embodied the Doctor's blood and body no longer in the world, but worthy to be praised all the same. Daily, as more visitors came, the shrine expanded, now covering the entire cracked sidewalk to the road along where the courthouse used to be.

From the dumpster, the young girl had witnessed many people come and go, posting photos with contact information on the telephone pole of loved ones and friends who had gone missing during the war with the alien creatures. Letters, poems, song lyrics, and other expressions of thanks and love for those who had died during the conflict and for Doctor Gombya lay damaged from the rain among the burnt out candles, dead flowers, and soggy teddy bears. Many words, particular to the Doctor, wished him a blessed afterlife.

And now, three days since the invasion, with the lid of the dumpster slightly raised, during one of those strange sunshowers where the sun shined through a light rain, Hannah watched the woman reach out of the car, pick up a burned out candle off the curb, and take it inside the vehicle. The square ship, still lit and hovering over Kampala, continued to provoke fear over the otherwise mournful scene.

The woman had visited before and had been the first to visit the shrine since the heavier rain had moved out. As a light rain fell solemnly, a flame grew inside the car. Seldom it moved. Humming sounded out of the vehicle; a melody Hannah swore she had heard before. Perhaps from a church or a distant memory of her mother, she didn't know. Its notes and the rain hitting the lid of the dumpster made her want to come out of hiding and join the woman in the car.

The rain stopped, leaving a filmy, reflective coating in the sunlit air like looking at life through a bubble. The flame moved in the car, disappeared, and then reappeared again outside the opened car door. The burning candle was set down from where it had been taken, holding all of the promise that other candles would be lit again and the fires of Earthling's spirits would burn once more.

Peeking out from under the dumpster lid, Hannah began to cry. It was as if the rain had stopped over Kampala and now rained out of her eyes. She had grown tired of caring for herself when no one else in the world had. Dying alone would be worse than death itself, so the only way to avoid the experience was to stay alive.

Hannah felt for the woman, the people of Uganda, and the rest of the world. Despite having nothing, this young girl hadn't lost everything—compassion being one of them. If anyone had a right to be mad at the world, it was her. But not today. All of those people, who had come to the shrine, bearing gifts and, especially, the woman in the car had somehow helped the young girl regain some courage. Going it alone for so long had been tough and she knew she had to meet the woman.

Waste crusted and smelly, the girl climbed out of the dumpster. For some reason, it had only occurred to her then that she could have left it at any time. Ending it all wouldn't have been so bad—at least it would end. But those moments dying alone—her last moments—was something to avoid altogether. Hope there would be someone someday kept her hanging on.

The car door was closing, so she ran. Burned out candles, dead flowers, soggy teddy bears sprawled out over the sidewalk didn't leave any room for her, so she ran up to the passenger door, hoping the woman would see her before pulling away.

Standing outside the passenger door, Hannah stared into the car. The woman inside stared back, having seen the girl run there. Finally, the passenger window rolled down. Odors of the dumpster, urine, and near-death body odor rolled into the car. The woman didn't react to it. Instead, she understood it.

Hannah asked the woman if she could light a candle and the woman reopened her door, retrieved an unlit candle beside her lit one from the curb, and handed it to the girl through the passenger door window along with a means of lighting it. The girl lit it and the woman, reverently, moved the burning candle through the car and set it down beside her own.

"What's your name?" the lady asked and the girl replied, "Hannah. What's yours?" Proudly, the woman answered, "Annrita Gombya, Doctor Park Gombya's wife." Seeing the name meant nothing to the girl, Mrs. Gombya continued, "This shrine is for the Doctor—my husband." Now, the girl understood and, hesitantly, said, "I saw it."

There was no question now, intuition had given Annrita understanding and the stench of the girl, although repulsive, just might contain a remnant of rawness of her husband's death. It took her a moment to let go any imagination of it and then said, "You don't know what happened, do you?" Hannah looked up at the hovering spaceship, then at Annrita, and shook her head she didn't.

"Do you have a place to go?" Annrita asked. "Someone to care for you?" Again, the young girl shook her head she didn't, so Annrita said, "You do now," as she leaned over and pushed open the passenger door. The Kampala rain returned to Hannah's eyes as she got in the car. Conditions that cause it to rain are understood. Tears, on the other hand, can come out of joy, pain, or no reason at all.

As Annrita pulled away from her husband's shrine, she told the girl what had happened. How her husband had called from the office to explain what he was going to try— and to say goodbye. At the rate the aliens devoured humans, the Molecular Virologist guessed if someone didn't act fast, it wouldn't be long before the human race became extinct.

He had decided to inject himself with the Ebola virus he had brought in the special briefcase from the breakout in Liberia, Africa and hoped that by being eaten by a group of aliens that they would, in turn, become infected and spread the virus between themselves on the ground and carry it with them back to their ships. He had asked his wife to contact a specific scientist he had just worked with in Liberia, for him to spread the word and have the process duplicated all over the world. Self-giving sacrifice by others would need to be acted upon for this to work.

All over the world, humans had volunteered to serve humanity. Exceptional people with a sense of calling, the same calling Doctor Gombya had heard, to venture into danger or at least willing to enter it where many others would run away. He had counted on it. The hardest part would entail getting the Ebola virus, all strains, to people willing to infect themselves.

Despite questions of its validity, the Hail Mary worked much faster than Park would have guessed. If the disease took one to two weeks to kill off the aliens, that would have been too long, and humans would be extinct; if the virus would have any effect at all. With the aliens being organic life forms, the same as humans, the disease went to work inside them and on their immune systems. Blood leaked. Organs failed. And, ultimately, germs, which most humans had become immune, had entered their defenseless forms and caused chaos.

Within forty-eight hours, news reports broadcasted that every alien on the ground had died. Aerial footage of the carnage from all over the world showed aliens sprawled everywhere among the destruction. There were minimal signs of human remains among them. Surviving Earthlings understood why. Death had interrupted their meals.

No one knew for sure about the aliens in the odd crafts still hovering over every capital and major city of the world. But as attacks from those ships slowed and eventually ceased, it was reasonable to conclude the virus had destroyed all aliens aboard the hovering spacecrafts.

It was believed that devastation to buildings and other physical assets most likely would never have occurred if it weren't for the viral attack waged against the aliens. At least, initially, they had come to feast. Destroying infrastructure might inadvertently destroy humans and for them to do that wouldn't make sense.

Of course, no one knew for sure, if the aliens had any intent on destroying the Earth once its inhabitants had been wiped from the face of it. Was there an interest in the planet? Had they come in totality or were more on the way? Time would reveal the unknown and perhaps, one day, the technology in their spaceships would provide answers and be useful.

Until then, *Rejoice!* For the Molecular Virologist, Doctor Park Gombya, and others like him, who had sacrificed themselves to arguably the worst way of dying by being eaten alive, had saved humanity from extinction—with less than a billion people to spare.

Nearly seven billion people of all ages from every lot in life had their bodies consumed by the alien creatures. Now, survivors needed to be careful in cleaning up the world and watchful of infected hosts. Never, in the history of the world, had there ever been an Ebola breakout spanning the entire globe. This Earthbound killer still might annihilate humans from the face of the Earth—just as the aliens had intended.

THUNDER rumbled outside. Lightning flashed through the tiny metal French-paned window into the small bathroom. With the electric out on the block, Rennis saw his reflection appear in the cracked mirror for a second, then shade over into a silhouette.

Leaning both hands on the crack-repaired porcelain sink, he stared at the black form in the mirror, as water dripped out of the spigot. His caucasian hands weren't white anymore. Usually, their pale white skin appeared light-colored even in the dark. Sometimes, over the summer, when he had a tan going, they would appear darker than usual, but this time of year, end of October, the tan had faded and he was white again.

Wherever he touched, black smears marked the white sink and streaked down the inside to the drain where the drip dropped.

The bathroom walls and ceiling were a dark-green color, but in the darkness, they looked black. Rennis welcomed the blackened color, which was way better than having to look at possibly the ugliest green on Earth. It wasn't hard to figure out why Mr. Russel, the owner and manager of the apartment building, had used the paint. Had to be a government leftover where they had overordered and overpaid, then gave it away.

How could Mr. Russel not take the paint and put it to use? Free was free, so the cheapskate most likely took what they allowed and used it immediately before they wanted it back. Stupid to think such a thing, but Mr. Russel had.

At least according to a long-time tenant, Mr. Simms, who had told his first hand account to Rennis shortly after he and Stacia had moved in. Russel offered tenants in the building a two-day grace period on any month's rent for whoever painted at least five bathrooms, including theirs. Simms said he had declined because he would never need the grace period and thought the offer was grossly unfair.

But, many in the building participated, including several husbands and wives, so they would gain a four-day grace period in their back pocket instead of two.

Which was okay with Mr. Russel, as long as he didn't have to shell out any money for this operation, he could wait another forty-eight to ninety-six hours to receive rental payments. No biggie. A delay was only a delay. And if they couldn't pay, then they couldn't stay.

Mr. Simms said when the painters had shown up to paint his bathroom, he thought there might be some cleanup involved, sanding and such to at least remove the mold spots from the surface of the walls.

Well, of course, they didn't. Essentially, they were

working for free, so no one was willing to go the extra mile. Even if they wanted to, Russel would have squashed it. He always cut corners like that to save a buck and time. So, they painted right over the mold holding the walls together and upright.

That was nearly forty years ago, now.

The diarrhea-green paint made Rennis envision prior tenants using the ceiling and walls to wipe their asses and it repulsed him every time he entered, refusing to touch the walls.

But it wasn't just the bathroom that pissed Rennis off to the highest pissing. It was the entire goddamn apartment. Which only passed as an *apartment* in the most rudimentary terms. And how it passed inspections was anyone's guess. The entire godforsaken building should be condemned to hell.

But, Rennis had a theory on that. Low-income housing automatically made everything else associated with it *low*. Low rent came in, so, in order for Mr. Russel to make a profit, expenditures were kept low; thus, shoddy repairs, puke-green painted bathrooms, and an inspection threshold so low it was impossible to fail.

And low rent also meant a puny apartment with few rooms. The more rooms, the tinier they had to be. Especially in the city.

Angered, Rennis gripped the sides of the sink. His hands slipped on the porcelain—from all of the blood on them.

From living in this apartment, he had formed a slight case of claustrophobia. And those diarrhea-green walls and ceiling with their mold and fecal smears from asses being wiped on them closed in on him. To touch him with their filth.

Only one person could be in there at a time as it was without the walls and ceiling shrinking it further.

Of course, the bathroom wasn't really shrinking. These realistic episodes came more frequently lately as Rennis' fear of confined spaces intensified over the last year.

But when they happened, they were real to him. And these episodes happened mostly in the bathroom, the smallest room in the apartment.

Don't blame Rennis. Blame the perpetual shrunken state of the bathroom. The damn toilet stuck out into the area in front of the sink and anyone sitting on it could reach out and touch the edge of the bathtub without their ass-cheeks ever leaving the seat.

Once, when Rennis and his wife, Stacia, had first moved in, his wife had come in to use the toilet while he was at the sink, shaving. What a fucking disaster. His back hurt like a motherfucker from avoiding his wife's legs while leaning sideways to see in the damn mirror. A cracked mirror, by the way, as in cracks, which made matters worse, because, of course, the largest unbroken section of mirror was to the side nearest the toilet.

Even now, alone in the bathroom, Rennis' right leg touched the front of the bowl. That's not all. That would only be half of it. The side of his left leg was touching the side of the bathtub.

Now, don't go thinking of one of those bathtubs large enough to lie down in. This tub wasn't anything near that size. Cut it in half or into thirds. About the size of a utility sink. Nothing more than a shower base with a taller than usual wall to step over.

That's how tight the fucking bathroom was. Unfit for average-sized people and height didn't matter. Midgets with any kind of girth would suffer the same issues. No, the only type of people Rennis could think of that would do alright in here were stick-people—not true, ghosts would fair better—both of which he knew didn't exist. Anorexics and small children were probably the best-suited human-types for such a small space, but even they would have problems in here. Especially if one of them were sprawled on the floor, puking an offering into the porcelain god's offering bowl.

From then on, a rule had been established between Rennis and his wife: only one person could be in the bathroom at a time. The only way they could both be in there *and fit* was if someone was in the shower, while the other used the mirror, sink, or toilet.

That was just the bathroom. Onto the kitchenette. Any word ending in *ette* was a polite way of saying *small*. No guy wants his manhood to be referred to as a dick*ette*. Nowadays, no woman, who happened to have one, either.

But calling the puny kitchenette anything else would be inaccurate. It was a small kitchen. About as wide as a recliner, although Rennis seriously doubted a recliner would fit. Many times, it had crossed his mind to test his theory, but then feared he might not get the damn chair back out. Then what would they do?

Climb over it every time they needed to get to the refrigerator is what. And they couldn't use the oven or lower cabinets either. It would render that area useless, which they couldn't afford.

Similar to the bathroom, all it took was two people to be in the kitchenette at the same time to jam it up. Forget moving around normally when there was another person in there. Shoulder-to-shoulder didn't work, because they would be too wide. Ridiculous. Passing each other required a side-shuffle. Yes, turning the shoulders and stepping sideways like waddling penguins.

Believe it or not, Rennis and Stacia had moved into the place for many reasons, but one of them, a main one, was so they had—drumroll please—*more room*.

Seriously? But it was true. They had rented a single room, a bedroom, before this place. When the rent for it damned-near approached this apartment, it was a no-brainer.

Stacia was so excited. She had told Rennis she had felt like they were moving up in the world. Things were turning in their favor. All they had to do was keep going and believe everything was going to turn out alright.

Not Rennis. He believed they must be dumbasses to move in here. He hated the apartment when they had toured it. When the tour had ended, in what seemed like seconds, he looked at Mr. Russel and asked, *'Where's the rest of the apartment?'*

Before answering, Russel looked at Rennis, then at Rennis' wife. She was glowing, precisely what he had wanted to see. So, looking at her, he came off with, "It's enough for another interested couple who wants it. And they even have kids."

Rennis told him, "They can have it," and headed for the door, while his excited wife blurted, "We'll take it!"

Back to the kitchenette. The *side-step-pass*—sounds like a line-dance—only lasted so long. Right up until Stacia became pregnant and started to show. Which was the nice way of saying she ballooned. No bigger. Like a blimp. Rennis never knew the human body could expand like that.

It wouldn't be right or fair to have *Goodyear* painted on his wife somewhere, because it hadn't been a good year. Not even close. And with another year coming and their first child on the way, next year might be worse—but they sure would be a tight-knit family in this *apartment.*

Which brings us to the bedroom. Oh, that's right—there wasn't a fucking bedroom! They slept on a pull-out bed in the couch in the living room. Every ass-licking night, they had to pull that thin-mattressed, uncomfortable bed out of the sofa and unfold it flat, so they had something to sleep on. And when the damn thing was out all the way, there was barely any space in the room to move around. Getting in and out of bed was like tight-roping a thin ledge along the wall.

If it had been a ledge, Rennis would have jumped off a long time ago. Only, the *apartment* was on the first floor. Go figure. Where every noise imaginable of people coming in and going out of the apartment building could be heard through the walls as if the walls weren't there.

As far as the city, forget about it. Everything sounded the same in the *apartment* as if standing outside on the sidewalk. Rennis knew for he had tried it once.

This place wasn't fit for grown-ups to live in, let alone

children. Yelling, swearing, slapping, screwing, and banging all sounded as if they had happened inside *their* apartment. Tenants carried on like they had privacy. If no one could see them, then no one could hear them.

Wrong! Rennis' wife knew everything about everybody. Conversations happening in the apartments around their's came through so clean and crisp, it was like she was part of it.

Interesting stuff. And just about every night, she updated Rennis on what she had heard. Usually, he wasn't in the mood to hear about other people's lives. Didn't care whether they lived or died, although it would be a hell of a lot quieter if they weren't there.

But not owning a television or radio, his wife's eavesdropping was the only entertainment around. Sure, some nights, Rennis would eat dinner, then venture out into the city to waste the night away. But, it was cheaper to just throwback a few beers at the *apartment* and listen to his wife ramble. Most of it he could care two-shits about, but, once in a while, something would be going on that he found quite interesting. Especially after a few beers were in him.

Mindful of what they knew about others, Rennis and his wife had vowed to keep their conversations to a whisper in the apartment. Rule number two had been established. More rules followed, but this might have been the most important. A wailing baby was going to draw enough attention as it was.

And when the baby had come, oh *boy*, it had. This little guy had the lungs of an opera singer. Long and short wails came out like notes of songs Rennis' wife swore she recognized. Which made matters worse. Because, sometimes, instead of quieting the baby, she let it whine— and would sing to it.

Death threats from pissed-off tenants shouted through the front door, through the walls, and down through the ceiling. And not just because of the baby crying either.

Except one evening, rule number two had been violated

by Rennis when he had stormed into the apartment, ranting and raving about how he had lost his job. He was too pissed to care about rule number two or others complaining about the noise. Let them say something or, better yet, come near him. He was already in the swing of things, as in fist and feet flying into the wall. Better that than his wife and kid. Not that anyone in this building would have reported it if Rennis was beating on his family.

When he had finished punching and kicking the wall, so much of it was missing that he stood there, looking into the adjoining apartment's living space, seeing white lines on a cheap-mirrored coffee table, and some broad jerking her man's limp, while he snorted a line in one inhale like a vacuum.

Oh, yes, the godforsaken lives of the lowest of the low in one of the raunchiest places on Earth. So low that a bathroom, living space, and kitchenette rated being called an *apartment*. Shit, college snobs have better dorm rooms than this hellhole. Even prison inmates enjoy better living conditions sometimes, especially at the white-collar joints.

Worse yet, Mr. Russel had tacked up a measly, couple-dollar tarp between the apartments. It remained that way for nine months. Fine. Let those druggies listen to a crying baby.

Mr. Russel required the assistance of Rennis in fixing the wall if he didn't want his rent raised. Of course, Rennis didn't after losing his job, so he helped. When it was finished, it looked fine. But appearances can be deceiving. And this was. Because the material Mr. Russel had used didn't block the sound any better than the tarp that had been up.

At least their visual privacy was back. Not that Rennis or his family had a lot to worry about when it came to security because they owned very little. What they owned was in the apartment and the apartment wasn't big enough to hold very much. They couldn't afford storage and what money came in went right back out—sometimes before it came in, especially with Rennis working part-time gigs, never landing a full-time job.

That's how it went for a little more than a year, scraping by on Rennis' part-time wages. And just when he insisted Stacie find work, she showed him the results of an at-home pregnancy test. Nine months later, they had a baby girl.

Seven years flew by and they still lived in that fucking *apartment*. Jobs came and went. Summers without vacations. Birthdays without much partying. And holidays without celebration.

But it's okay. Hellish living was over. Because, as Rennis leaned against the sink hardly big enough to piss in— something he had commented frequently—his wife's body laid on the floor in the dark kitchenette. Across it actually, with her lower legs and feet punched through the cabinet doors under the sink and her head and shoulders inside the fridge.

Don't ask Rennis how she got that way. If he had the chance to kill her again, he doubted she would end up like that the second time, even if he tried.

The authorities were going to have one hell of a time trying to figure out her cause of death. Because, when his wife had opened the fridge to start moving the little in it up to the freezer in hopes of preserving it until the electricity returned, he came up from behind and thumped her head with a saucepan full of uncooked rice.

He had walloped her so hard, that the pan vibrated in his hand until it dislodged, landing between their feet on the linoleum floor. Rice flew everywhere. He would have liked to have said *just like on our wedding day*, but couldn't. If he had, it would be a lie. And lying at that particular moment seemed wrong.

Blunt-force trauma to the head was going to be a slam-dunk for the authorities to figure out. The bumps on her head would be a *dead* giveaway. Yes, bumps. Because he had also hit her head with whatever he could get his hands on nearby before she fell. Which wasn't right away. Being married to her for so long, he knew she could be hard-

128

headed at times, but that was ridiculous.

In a fury, he just grabbed whatever he could get his hands on. And whatever he had gotten ahold of went straight to his wife's head.

Instead of bending down to pick up the saucepan, he got a hold of the frying pan on the stove. Slices of bologna flew out of it like frisbees when he swung it and when it hit his wife's head, it sang like a church bell on Sunday morn.

And dented, that's how cheap it was—probably made in China or some fucking sloped-head, slanted-eyed place like that. Not cast iron, either. *Oh, no.* That surely would have killed her.

That second blow had sent his wife forward against the fridge, wedged between the opened door and its chest.

This hard-headed broad was still standing.

So, he hit her again with the frying pan. The handle broke off in Rennis' hand; that's how much of a piece of shit it was. Discount store crap, because they couldn't afford anything better. The pan clanged on the saucepan on the floor.

He had reached for something else, but couldn't remember now, because it wasn't needed. As his wife fell to the floor in what seemed like slow-motion, he followed her down and stabbed the handle into her stomach. That was when her feet had come out from under her and crashed through the cabinet doors under the sink as if she were a karate expert. Her head and shoulders had no other place to go except into the fridge. Width-wise, there wasn't the floor space for her body to fit in that direction any other way.

The handle didn't penetrate easily, but it went in. Not much at first. Not until Rennis had gotten to his feet, found the toaster, and rammed it down on the handle sticking out of her stomach.

Good thing he had held it at the ends because the handle poked through one side of the toaster and nearly came out the other, raising a bump in the lower-grade metal. The only reason it didn't was because the handle had sunk deeper into his wife.

Maybe that was what he had started to grab next—the toaster: that or a rusted metal bread bin on the counter. As he knelt, looking down at his wife, the smell of bologna and beef rice had filled his nostrils.

Standing at the bathroom sink, now, he could still smell it. The aroma of whatever they had cooked had always filled and lingered in the apartment. Funny how the paper-thin walls couldn't drown-out sound, but they sure could retain odors.

He hated bologna and rice; they had eaten it so often. When he had seen it scattered all over the kitchen, he felt relieved he wouldn't be eating it for the umpteenth time in however many days. He used to keep track of such things, then gave up on it about the same time he had given up on a lot of things—eventually, life.

It didn't matter.

When Rennis had knelt beside his wife's body, he scooped some rice off the floor and stuffed it into her gaping mouth. A slice of bologna followed, stuffed in by a finger—a quick bite for the road.

That was when the kids had appeared in the kitchenette entrance, wearing their Halloween costumes.

At first, they stared at the scene—their father kneeling beside their mother and the kitchenette a mess. It was dark, but not that dark to not see the lay of the situation.

Mother didn't move.

Then, the girl, age seven, asked, "Are we still going trick-or-treating?"

She was dressed as a female pop-star. Someone his wife and daughter had said when they had seen it in the store, but Rennis didn't know who it was or care to remember. All he cared about was the costume had been cheap. One of those ten-dollar jobbies from the discount store they used to shop at. Same for the boy's.

Age nine, the boy focused on what he saw in the kitchenette, namely his still mother, not on trick-or-treating.

For the whites of his eyes glistened in the darkness like hollowed pearls, which examined her from afar.

Mom still hadn't moved.

"What are you doing to mom?" the boy asked. "Is she okay?"

Rennis stared at his son.

Even in the dark, the boy knew by the whites of his father's eyes.

Rennis knew his son could see him because the boy's eyes twitched as he cowered.

Rennis looked down at his wife, then back at his son, and said, "Sure, buddy. She'll be fine. She just slipped is all."

"Do you need help getting her up?" the boy asked.

"I suppose I could use a little help," the father said. "But first, why don't we order a pizza."

"Oh, my God," the girl said, shocked, then yelled, *"piiiizzaaa!"*

Eyeing his boy, the father asked him, "You know where the number is?"

"Sure," the boy said. "On the inside cover of the phone book."

"You know your last name, don't you?"

"Yeah, it's…"

Rennis raised both hands with their index fingers pointing up. "*Uh, uh, uh.* I know what our last name is."

At that moment, light shined through the front-window curtains into the tiny apartment and peeked over the counter, which divided the living room from the kitchenette, onto Rennis' raised hands. Both kids stepped back because a glossy liquid coated them.

The father noticed their strange reaction, then followed their eyes to his hands. The light scanned across the walls then disappeared, rendering the apartment darker than it had seemed before it came. Probably a bus, pulling into the stop in front of the apartment building.

Looking at them, Rennis said, "From the bologna."

"Now," he continued, looking at his son and lowering his

hands, "you know our address?" Shaking his head, he added, "Don't tell me—I know that, too."

"I think so," the boy said.

"You're a big boy. Why don't you call and order a large cheese for delivery. Can you do that?"

"I think so. I heard mom do it once."

"And, if you forget your last name or our address, just grab one of those bills addressed to us on the end table. It's sure to be right."

"Large cheese," the boy said, making sure.

"That's what I said," Rennis said, faking a smile.

"*Um*, what do I do, daddy," the girl asked.

"You know your numbers?"

"*Daddie!* I'm seven."

"All right, smartypants, then help your brother dial the number."

"I get to touch the phone?"

"*Sure*, why not. Live a little."

"And press the buttons?"

"Only the ones needed to place the call. Your brother will tell you which ones to press with that pudgy little finger. So, do you want pizza or not?"

"I do! I do!" the little girl said, while her brother nodded.

"Then, call it in," their father said.

The girl hop-skipped to the phone, while her brother remained. From what he could tell, Mom hadn't moved or made a sound. How her body had gotten lodged like that, feet through the cabinet doors under the sink and her head inside the refrigerator, was beyond him. It didn't look right. Wasn't right. Nor was his father.

Not knowing what to do or say, he slowly turned and walked toward the phone without the same enthusiasm as his sister.

As soon as the boy had left his sight, Rennis' face blanked. The commotion of the kids' bickering back-and-forth was nothing more than background noise of his own thoughts. He stood, looked down at his dead wife, and walked into the living room. The boy held the receiver to an ear, while the girl shined a flashlight down on the opened phonebook.

"Dad," the boy said, "the call won't go through."

Rennis took the receiver, listened, then placed it in its cradle to hang up. He removed the flashlight from the girl's hand and turned it off.

"Aren't we getting pizza?" the girl asked.

That was the last thing Rennis remembered.

Now, as he leaned on the sink in the bathroom, his hands were bloodier than they were in the kitchenette after killing his wife. So much so, they adhered to the porcelain. Which was fine, because it helped in keeping him upright.

Whatever had happened earlier, a transformation had taken place inside him right before all hell had broken loose. It had broken free in the kitchenette. That much he knew.

Impossible to prove, all he could say for sure was he felt different. Wasn't himself. But, it was more than a feeling. Something physical. As if a section of his brain had woken from a spellbinding slumber, sparked by hell's fire, which had ignited a buried part of him to life, freeing hell from its long captivity. Hell manifested through Rennis on the Earth, full of anger, hatred, malice, and more from waiting and knowing it wouldn't be free for long because its time was short.

Which meant it was there all along, waiting, stewing, and crazed from cabin-fever.

That was the best he could describe it. For he knew in part, yet knew nothing.

Now that what he had done was over, there was no question how he felt. *Free. Released from a long captivity.* And *detached.* From chains that had kept him in the pit. From family obligations. Bills stacked on the end table. Not having any money. Overpriced, poor-quality things in the apartment. The miniature apartment itself.

And the world.

Its laws and norms no longer ruled his existence. There

was no reason to continue to abide by them. No reason to try to fit in. No reason to fear them—or anyone.

For Rennis was fear itself. Embodied with it. Hell incarnate. From a lower plane, beneath mankind's feet, yet higher, where it had originated in the heavens, lifting him out of the world with angel's wings to a higher plane. Above the world and its ways. Not of the world, nor himself. A different man entirely. Not a man, more than a man. How he had gotten there, he didn't know. There was no need to know.

So, as he looked at the black silhouette of his head behind the cracks of the broken mirror, for the transformation to be complete, he needed a new identity and name. How he knew that or why he didn't know. But both needed to happen.

Water dripped out of the spigot. Its various uses were many. Nourishment. Agriculture. Farming. Cleaning. Yes, a cleansing. All of these applied to the physical world, but also in the spiritual.

Ah, there's the disconnect. Few question how water can cleanse sin. How baptisms were an outward sign a person had changed on the inside with nothing more than a few sprinkles of holy water. Heck, there was more water in the blood on Rennis' hands, let alone the crimson on his face and shirt than there were in some baptisms.

And there it was. True transformation required blood; Rennis knew that now. In part, anyway. Blood he could get. The rest, well, he would leave the particulars of how staining blood could cleanse and whiten to whatever had woken up inside him.

Fully immersed as a newborn baby coming out of the womb, Rennis' rebirth had begun and with it required a new identity—a new name.

And that new identity already existed, urging Rennis on to accept it as his own. By showering him with thoughts and feelings of what he could become. Showing him glimpses of a life without care, without need, without fear. *If*—he accepted.

Compelled by how this new self felt, Rennis accepted. Many times, it had crossed his mind to shed the old man—the only man. To extinguish himself without a replacement.

But, to his surprise, he didn't feel any different after accepting. For he had already taken on a new life back in the kitchenette. One without care, need, or fear. Killing his wife, instead of himself, had ushered in a force—a new soul perhaps—and he wasn't the same, yet he was.

His bloodied face in the mirror appeared dark. More like a darker man's than his own Caucasian. Only the whites of his eyes and teeth gave him reference it was a reflection of a face at all. His teeth showed from a gaped mouth on an elongated face, expressing shock, fear, and fulfillment that the day he had thought about so many times before had finally come, arriving in such a strange, unusual way he had never considered previously. Not like this, anyway.

A splatter of rain tapped the tiny window in the bathroom. Then more. And more. Sprinkles. Maybe baptism sprinkles, finally cleansing the world of all of its sins that so many had been waiting for. Raindrops tapped the window with soft knocks, wanting inside, wanting Rennis.

The oval whites of Rennis' eyes stared back at him out of the mirror. He swore his reflection had moved without him moving. More and more, that seemed to occur. It wasn't his reflection anymore, but another, a separate entity, a twin, miming his moves when he did move and moving how it wanted the rest.

The knocking on the windowpanes became louder, more intense, as the subtle rain turned into a downpour. Voices whispered from the window, calling him by name, *"Reeennis. Reeennis."*

That's how it starts, doesn't it? A faint whisper. Subtleties into downpours; some torrential.

Rennis turned and looked at the window. The dark green paint surrounding it appeared black with the electricity out. The glass panes grayed from a fog behind them, almost silver. Bulbous raindrops, clinging to the window, sparkled from bending light.

Until the drops weren't drops anymore.

Rennis didn't want to, but closed his eyes, giving them a rest, resetting them, so they would stop playing tricks on him this Halloween.

When he opened his eyes, they saw the same thing. They were there, real, tiny hands clapping the glass. No arms or any other body parts—just hands, smaller than a newborn baby's. Smaller than a premature newborn's. Even the smallest person who had ever lived didn't have hands this little.

They grew against the window, zooming in as on a computer screen. Rennis turned his body to face the window. In stumbling back from what he saw, there was no place to go in the green-shit bathroom. The back of his legs was already up against the bathtub. Struggling to stay upright, he grabbed the shower curtain. The damn thing couldn't hold him, bringing the rod down with it into the tub.

The things outside the window had grown larger since he had last seen them. But they weren't hands, nor things, for they had a name, and although he had lived in the city his whole life, he knew exactly what they were—hooves. Yes, black ovals with a V cut out of the top of them.

It was enough to weaken Rennis' knees and send him sitting in the tub. Something was underneath him—under the shower curtain and rod.

Quickly, he got to his feet and checked the window. Within streaked drops of rain and a silvery fog, blurred outlines of black hooves pressed against the glass. As if the devils and elements knew his eyes were upon them, the fog swirled in a blowing wind, rattling the window, and a driving rain sprayed against the glass. The hooves ran in place, sounding like a stampede.

But not of animals. That's *not* what Rennis saw. Yes, his physical eyes saw hooves, but his mind's eye saw them for what they were. Unimagined, so perhaps he had seen them through spiritual eyes. An unencumbered version from a different perspective.

And like most things spiritual, what he saw couldn't be explained although he could comprehend it. For although he was standing in the puny bathroom of his apartment, he wasn't either. Simultaneously physically in the world and spiritually taken to another place. A place with dry sand under his feet and surrounding him as far as his spiritual eyes could see.

Rennis stood in a barren desert, where sand grains in perfectly windblown undisturbed dunes twinkled like stars in the nighttime sky. Only it wasn't night. A royal blue sky without a cloud in it met the sand. Desolate. Peaceful. Simple.

Suddenly, a thunderous noise exploded behind him. He turned and saw a clouded stampede of black silhouettes coming over a dune toward him. He turned back and cowered, hearing them coming. A dust storm arrived ahead of them, whipping around him, then a rain.

Yes, a driving rain in the desert, that soaked Rennis to the bone as they ran by, a few of them brushing against him, but most of them had fanned out to go around.

Rennis wanted to look, but the stirring dust and driving rain were too much for his eyes. So, he remained still and waited.

A deafening sound rang his ears. He struggled to cover his eyes and ears adequately. Eventually, he settled on crossing his forearms over his eyes like a visor and covering his ears with his hands. They smelled like wet animals as they passed.

When they were far enough past him, he lowered his arms and opened his eyes in time to see the two paths converge once more into a single herd. But not a herd of animals. Not entirely. For they were bi-ped men in the form of men. Except for the thick hair covering their shins and calves below the knees—down to their hooves.

137

And they weren't running on desert sand. But smooth glass—like that of a window.

Neither was Rennis wet. Nor the sand under his feet. Not anymore. For it was dry as ash—under the hooved legs he stood on.

When Rennis looked up, he was back inside the bathroom once more, facing the fogged-over window. Thin silver strands of rain shimmered now and again within the fog on the other side, behind black bottoms of hooves—marching—those bi-ped men he had seen who were animals from the knee down.

Rennis checked his legs. Blue work pants covered them and the tops of his workboots. Then, the slacks and boots faded away, leaving his legs and feet bare.

Funny, they don't feel naked.

There was nothing to laugh at when two senses, touch and sight, were out of sync. The disconnect between the physical world and what Rennis perceived brewed a sickening stir in the pit of his stomach.

Hair rapidly grew out of his legs below the knee; it wasn't long before they were covered. His feet darkened and shriveled as if decaying rapidly; excruciating pain from breaking bones and torquing flesh cramped not only his feet but his entire body. To his amazement, they had compressed into hard, black hooves.

Unable to look at his animal legs any longer, Rennis looked up, the window unchanged.

"We're all animals."

It sounded like his own voice, but he never spoke. Hadn't for a while. Not since he had told his kids to, *"...call it in,"*—for the pizza that is.

"You're being called, Rennis. Incoming call."

Rennis turned toward the mirror where the voice had sounded. A reflection of himself was in it. But not how it should be in reflecting how Rennis stood. No, the reflection faced out of the mirror—smiling.

"Call it in," the reflection said. "For you were made a

little higher than animals and a little lower than angels. You were made from both, Rennis."

Rennis went for the bathroom door, but it slid closed; one of those sliding doors tucked inside the wall because it was the only door that would work in such a tight space.

Something grabbed his leg, so he looked. There was nothing. A flash of lightning entered through the tiny window, enough for him to see sticking out from under the shower curtain—limbs—small ones—his children's.

The hooves smashed through the window, bringing in more rain and wind than the tiny window and angle should allow. But, it came in. As did lightening's light. And, as Rennis turned to see what was happening, rain sprayed and wind blew forcefully against him. Legless hooves flew toward him. Voices yelled his name, *"Reeennis! Reeennis!"*

Something grabbed the back of his calves. When he looked down, he saw the pale, youthful hands of his children—the sleeves of their costumes a *dead* giveaway.

Turned, looking past his shoulder, Rennis saw what he wished he hadn't. Two rounded bumps pressed up on the shower curtain. Their heads, he knew. As if the kids had changed their minds and decided to go trick-or-treating as ghosts instead.

And they were, haunting their father.

"Mom says you killed her, daddy," his son's voice said. *"Why?"*

"Tricks, daddy," his daughter said. *"It's all tricks and no treats."*

Through the children's grip on the back of his legs, Rennis felt a strange surge of vengeful determination enter him. Their vengeance. Immediately, he knew it was the lifeforce that had resurrected his children from death.

A violent grab, tug, and pull of Rennis' hair on the top of his head spun him back toward the mirror. His reflection had him. His clone. Perhaps, his evil twin. Controlling Rennis by the head with an arm and hand extending out of the mirror.

Rennis grabbed the arm with both hands to try to get it off him. Impossibly, he felt the pressure and strength of his own grips on his own arm as if he had grabbed himself.

But, unlike himself, the reflection's arm felt abrasive to the touch, similar to fiberglass, how touching it irritates the bare skin, causing the tiniest of cuts, but many. And grainy, like the sand used to make the mirror.

"Yeah," Rennis' reflection said, enjoying the onslaught on his flesh-and-blood. "Why did you kill your wife?" The reflection smiled.

Before Rennis could answer, those tiny hooves flew right into the side of his head. There was no pain where they had entered. Instead, his brain seized inside, trampled by animal hooves on the lower legs of men from his vision.

A one-way wind drove the rain sideways against him, soaking and chilling him in the worse combination.

An unrelenting tug of his hair and shake of his head had turned the reflection's smile into a gnashing of teeth.

Through them, the man in the mirror yelled, *"Huh? Answer! Why torment the boy more than he already is? Think of your daughter."*

Rennis rolled his eyes toward the bathtub. The two heads of his children underneath the shower curtain were taller now.

From beyond, the boy asked, *"Why, dad?"*

"And no more tricks, daddy," the girl scolded.

"I, ugh..." Rennis started.

Then, a yank of his hair straightened his body and silenced him.

As the reflection, somehow alive as its own entity, fisted a handful of Rennis' hair, it reached its other hand out of the mirror toward the sink. Veins bulged in Rennis' neck as he tried moving his head in the opposite direction, despite worsening the pain upon himself. No matter how much Rennis fought to free himself, he couldn't. Unbelievably, he felt his feet leave the floor.

A flash of dull gray whizzed across his face. A sting

followed. At first, it felt like his whole face had been stung. Then, it concentrated on his left cheek.

As soon as he had felt the pain, everything went still. The chaos over; stopped just like that.

Lightning flickered into the bathroom. Rennis stared into the mirror. A reflection of himself, perfectly transposed, stared back at him. He was smiling at himself—just as the reflection had done.

But the other reflection he had seen was gone, no longer pulling his hair or asking him why he had killed his wife.

In Rennis' raised hand was a butter knife, bloody, and close to his sliced left cheek.

Another light flashed into the bathroom, drawing his attention to the window. It was intact. Nothing on it but tiny rain globes. No hands or hooves. And no voices, whispering or yelling his name.

A passing glance across the mirror confirmed it was indeed his reflection as it should be, then settled on the shower. Its curtain hung from the rod, closed, as it had been before.

With the butter knife raised in his right hand, he grabbed the shower curtain in his left and slid it open. Lightning strobed intermittent flashes of light onto the tub—and the bodies of his dead children, still in their costumes.

After only a moment's pause, he turned back to the mirror, leaving the shower curtain open. While staring at himself—his reflection—a knowledge, only revealed once in a blue moon, enlightened him of the fact that he wasn't staring at *himself*, for he wasn't himself. Hadn't been since attacking his wife in the kitchenette.

Maybe some of his *self* had died before today—a slow death over the years. Then, more of him had died today with his wife and nearly the rest with his children, his last and only meaningful creations.

Which left *him*. The remnant of his true being.

Not much remained. So, only seeing *him* in the mirror, as if referring to another person—all part of the detachment—

Rennis brought the butter knife close to his face, pressed its grooved blade edge against his other cheek, and scraped it across it.

A crude cut resulted.

Despite the pain, he never winced. It was like watching it happen to someone else—and it was perfect.

The butter knife clanked in the sink when he dropped it. The face being *cut-up* wasn't someone else's, but his own and the pain came all at once. A stinging like he had never felt before. Like a bunch of bees had flown in there and attacked that catacomb with a vengeance. Not honey bees, but blood-thirsty bees. Surgery being performed without a painkiller.

But he had something for that. Something that he had kept hidden from his wife for years. A bottle of moonshine stashed on top of one of the kitchenette cabinets. His wife never dusted up there because she couldn't reach it. And if she couldn't reach it, it wasn't being dusted—nor the bottle found.

Yes, moonshine. A woman in the apartment building dated a guy who worked on a farm outside the city. He stole grain from his employer and boiled the shit right in his apartment located at the other end of the city. How the two of them had found each other in this big city blew Rennis' mind. It was no secret, though, the woman got around. Apparently, as far as the other side of the city. From what Rennis could tell, they seemed perfect for each other. The guy supplied the shine and she provided the heinie and whine.

High-proof stuff, too. The shine that is, the ass and whine not so much. But the moon was just what Rennis needed. No man could put up with what he had endured all of those years without it. Fuck, when things don't go your way and you see other people become famous and rich, well, you need something to cope, something that makes you relax and not give a damn about your lot in life—about that shaft in your cakehole.

No wonder there are so many suicides. When youthful

ignorance gives way to the sudden shock experienced at an unspecified age of realization that "Holy fuck! This is my life?" moment, living the rest of it out tends to seem pointless.

There it was, just where he had left it atop the cabinet. He brought the bottle down and stepped off his wife's dead body, which he had used as a stepping stool to reach it.

On top of the cabinet above the refrigerator was the safest spot to hide it because the fridge stuck out. If his wife had ever gotten the gumption to clean up there, she would probably skip above the fridge because it would be the hardest to reach for her.

Dust had collected on the bottle and he tried recalling the last time he had hit it up. Must have been a while, a couple of weeks maybe. The scrape of the cap unscrewing and *walla!* astronaut fuel to send him straight to the moon. Nasty tasting, but it worked like a potion. Not right away, of course. It took numerous sips followed by facial grimaces to get enough in him until he no longer felt the sting in his cheeks.

Like magic, really. It didn't take long until he felt numbed up enough to return to the bathroom sink, where he *cut-up* his face with the butter knife.

Shredded it, really. By the time he was done, his face pained as if the skin had been peeled off.

An accurate assessment. Very little skin remained on his face. More of his *self*, his identity, had been cut away, leaving only *him*, the true him underneath the façade, which no longer existed with his face removed. Putting on any kind of front no longer could be achieved without the skin over the face. Expressions could not be conveyed through the bloodied meat of a man, especially without lips.

Yes, everyone knows the lips' importance when it comes to facial expressions. Without lips, the mouth is useless in making them. Exposed teeth, as Rennis' were, never could convey a smile, frown, or any emotion. Think of a human skull, which looks the same every time. There's never any change; no expression of any kind.

By cutting up his face and removing most of his lips, Rennis had successfully removed his immediate identity. Not as deep as DNA or dental, but a layer. The important thing was, if he couldn't recognize his *cut-up* face in the mirror, then no one else would—as long as he changed clothes. Then the immediate identity transformation will be complete.

Physically, anyway, his outer shell, as long he kept his wallet at home. It would take DNA testing or dental records to identify him. Which would most likely mean he was dead. It didn't have to, of course, because those could be performed on any living person, but we all know those methods are usually reserved for the deceased.

The rest of his *self* had died with his family. No more jobs. Bills. Taxes. Anyone waiting for him or his money to show up will be waiting a long time. They will all think he had disappeared from the face of the Earth. Another Hoffa. Gerhart. One moment there, then where the hell are they?

No one would find him. No more usual spots. No more haircuts—unless he gave himself one. No more banking. No more unemployment line. No more apartment.

No one would care, he knew. One less person to collect bills from. One less worker the company would decide they no longer needed. Maybe not now, but, at some point, it was coming. As if his measly salary and benefits amounted to anything, let alone make or break a company. Both of which didn't amount to much. Little coming in and too much going out left him flat broke with nothing to show for his effort. They could all kiss his ass.

Where's that bottle?

Ah, yes. One thing Rennis had forgotten.

Returning to the kitchenette, he stepped over his wife, picked up the broken-handled frying pan, set in on the stove, and turned the burner on high.

One-by-one, he rummaged through the cabinets and found what he was looking for. He removed the lid of the container, tossed it aside, dug three fingers into the cooking grease, and flung it into the hot frying pan. Immediately, it sizzled, snapped, and popped. Heat and smoke rose from the pan to his exposed face.

Not caring, for he was free from care, he simply let go of the grease container and it dropped to the floor. Noticing it for only a moment, he wiped the grease off his fingers onto his shirt and returned to watching the hot pan.

A loud snap sounded. Rennis' chin pulsated as if it had been slapped. Then, a hot sting heated his entire bottom jaw. He grabbed the bottle of moonshine off the counter and poured a clear waterfall into his mouth.

> *Drown out the sorrow*
> *Live for tomorrow*
> *Same shit, different day*

Yes, *pour*—remember there were no lips to kiss the bottle. And without them, his accuracy was off. Not only had the shine burned his throat, but also his *cut-up* face, splashing on it like an aftershave. Much worse than the popped grease, air hitting where it shouldn't, or anything else so far.

Whoa! Rennis was feeling the effects now. *Whew, what a high!* Intense pain and one-hundred-percent proof moonshine had shot him to the moon. Exactly what he needed. The flesh of his face was starting to clot and harden in self-preservation. After another pour past his exposed teeth and down his throat—this time without a wasted drop—he set the bottle on the counter, stood in front of the stove, blew out a couple of breaths, and placed his fingertips into the hot oil, making sure they touched the bottom of the pan. They sizzled like bacon for a count of *One one-thousand. Two one-thousand. Three.*

Three didn't get its *one-thousand.* In a pained-panic, Rennis rushed to the sink, stepping on his wife to get there, and ran cold water over his cooked fingertips. Steam rose from them, that's how hot they were.

Relief never came to his darkened fingers. Not entirely. No matter how long he stood there, the tips of his fingers never felt soothed. They were damaged pretty good, seared on the outside and still cooking on the inside. Prints weren't the only things missing from them. Some flesh had melted off, too. As did a pinky nail, which had disappeared down the drain, exactly when, he wasn't sure.

Whatever. Just one of those things. Rennis had dealt with much worse.

Cuts may heal
But no matter how you feel
Inside cuts tend to stay

Still, he turned around, trampling on his wife to maneuver, opened the freezer—near-empty freezer—grabbed an ice tray, and popped some ice cubes into his hands. The old metal tray fell on his wife's breast. Not that she would feel it.

The ice cubes didn't help. They melted right away and weren't touching his fingertips, where they needed to.

But all wasn't bad. The crisp air soothed his butchered face, making the trip to the freezer worth it.

His fingers, on the other hand, still needed dealt with. They felt like mini-embers in a dying fire, still hot as hell, although they didn't look it. So, without hesitation, he placed his fingertips on the ice adhered to the bottom of the freezer and held them there. Which helped some, mostly from numbing them further on top of the alcohol.

When he went to scratch his head, his hands wouldn't move, because the tips of his fingers stuck to the ice crystals. The itch nagged his scalp and not being able to scratch it pissed him off. Growling and stretching his jaw to combat what felt like a biting bug on top of his head, he pulled his hands back with angered-strength. The freezer wouldn't let go—tug-of-war with a damn appliance. The compromised skin on his fingertips from having blood on them, been scorched in oil on the stove, cooled rapidly underwater, then placed on ice made them adherent, tacky like duct tape.

Rennis won the war. Sort of. His hands were free, but that was it. The burning in his fingertips seemed worse. Doubly-burned if that was possible. And it was. Stove-top burned in oil *and* freezer burned.

Fine. Rennis minded the pain but could care less about the appearance of his little embers, which now appeared pointed as if they had been sharpened in a pencil-sharpener, missing deep layers of skin and flesh. The freezer had them, mementos from their battle.

So, his fingertips matched his face now, exposed and unprotected. No biggie. Who knows, he might end up skinless by the time Halloween closed up shop for another year at midnight.

So be it—all part of the re-identification process. Only one thing remained: a change of clothes.

Leaving the water running in the sink, the freezer door open, and the ice tray on his wife, Rennis went to put on the final touch of his transformation.

When he entered the living space, the kids' masks laid on the ugly-patterned couch, along with their plastic pumpkins. He had grown-up using a pillowcase to collect his candy, but who couldn't part with ninety-nine cents for not one pumpkin but two they had bought last year after Halloween was over and stores tried clearing that stuff off the shelves for Christmas crap.

This wasn't how Rennis had planned on spending Halloween. Honest. Nor his family. They had other plans. His wife had been cooking dinner—blasted fried bologna and rice—so they could eat before heading out for trick-or-treating. In checking his watch, which was happening now. Almost seven o'clock, about halfway through.

While she cooked, the kids had gotten into their costumes, so when they had finished eating and cleaned up, they could go.

That was the plan, anyway.

Rennis picked up his daughter's mask. It was supposed to resemble some blonde-haired, white-girl singer. Hell, most of them are, aren't they? The big sellers. But who this one was supposed to be, he didn't know. His daughter knew— before.

His bloodied fingers ruined the mask. Smeared blood all over the girl's face as if she had just survived a cat-fight. Probably with another one of those richer-than-rich teens. Multi-millionaires by the time they graduated high-school.

What a fucked-up world.

With his other hand, Rennis picked up his son's mask. Who or what it was supposed to be, he couldn't tell. It looked like the face was supposed to be made out of metal, painted primarily red, with some black around the eyes. No imagination. They all looked like that.

It didn't matter. He would still use them. *How* wasn't clear, but it would come.

In less than five minutes, an idea on how to use them in his new digs had arrived. Another ten minutes went by and he was all set. It didn't look it, but he was. Wearing a pair of his wife's dirty undies he had pulled from the dirty clothes and the blonde-haired pop-singer mask over his crotch, held there by a clothespin in one eye, across the bridge of the nose, through the underwear, and clasped at the other eye. No imagination needed for what he was trying to say there. A statement for sure. Fitting for a weird night like Halloween. Still, a little bizarre for the weirdo he had become. Oh, yeah. Very much so.

He put on his work boots and tied them. That completed the bottom half.

The upper went just as easy. He put on an old orange t-shirt the kids had painted a face on last year so their daddy could dress up, too. At age six and eight, the kids had tried their best for good 'ole pops, but what a disaster. It only worked because it was for Halloween. One eye resembled a human eye, football-shaped, instead of the usual triangle cut out of most Jack-O-Lanterns, and off-kilter, like a football tilted on a tee, and painted pink by his daughter.

The other eye was never started because they had run out of time. A painted yellow dash for a nose. And the mouth wasn't anything more than black brushstrokes, running in every direction. The way it was done, the mouth was opened in spots and looked sewn in others, and ran the entire width of the shirt, like Charlie Brown's zig-zagged stripe on his shirts.

But, like any good father, he had worn it then and he wore it now. A tradition started last year.

And he didn't forget about his son's mask. No, he looped the string of the mask around his neck and had it facing backward. It was the only option. For he had created his own mask by cutting up his face.

And looking at what he could see of himself in the mirror, that is what remained on the surface. Without question, his identity had changed. A complete and utter transformation, inside and out. No one would ever see the inside change until it was too late, nor would anyone recognize his outside. He didn't and no one had been with him longer than he had himself.

Who he saw in the cracked mirror required a new name. A name to capture this night—Halloween. One that no one would ever guess, yet, every man shared. So, he would no longer go by his given name, Rennis Azurn Ebb. From now on, he would only be known as *Sinner*.

If anyone on Earth looked like sin, it was him. The *cut-up* face was one thing, but the missing lips and exposed teeth were nightmarish—a transgression against how any human should look.

Perhaps. But forget about the *cut-up* he had done to himself. What about cutting up his family? Their shells had been punctured and blood came out. Their lives cut down prematurely by his hands. Not in self-defense, but in malice.

Therefore, he was a Sinner, a name shared by all humans, for everyone had or will transgress in their own way by committing an immoral act that falls outside the boundaries of moral behavior or what most people consider basic good. Borderlines are usually blurred but are defined enough to render a judgment when the line had been crossed. It doesn't even have to be in the context of a divine law. Mortal law or norms can also be transgressed.

And he was okay with it. He would never have adopted the name Sinner if he wasn't.

He turned around and walked out of the tiny, diarrhea-green bathroom. No more cold showers. Cramped legs when taking a shit. None of it. It was all behind him now.

Including two children, left to rot in the shower. For they weren't *his* children any longer. Hadn't been, really, since his detachment, leading to theirs.

In entering the living space, he would never sleep on the pull-out couch again. Or have to listen to every goddamn noise as if it was happening right in his own living room.

In moving through the living space, he passed the kitchenette. The stove still on, freezer door open, refrigerator, too, with his wife's head and shoulders inside, her mid-section on the linoleum floor, and her legs and feet inside the cabinets under the sink.

Good riddance! To all of it. Let the place and the little in it burn. Everything that had happened between him and his wife had never resulted in much, so, in Sinner's mind, nothing lost.

Sinner opened the front door and walked out of the apartment, leaving the door open, and leaving behind a family and not much else, which some loser in life named Rennis had responsibility once—when he ruled the coop—before Sinner's arrival.

Fuck, Mr. Russell! Seeing that bastard first would be a real treat this Halloween, already knowing how he would kill the pole-smoker.

But, Sinner never felt compelled to seek him out. He had to leave. Head out to where the hooves were that had tapped the tiny window of his small bathroom. Out to where the voices had called him from. Into the rain to be baptized.

But, when Sinner exited the apartment building, no one was around; the sidewalk and street completely clear of another living soul.

Human soul, to be precise. A dog trotted by, ignoring him, not even interested in taking a sniff. Down the sidewalk, the herky-jerky movements of a quick cat caught his eye. What he had thought was another dog, sniffing a garbage can, looked to be a little roly-poly, and was, because it wasn't a dog at all, but a pig. Every city has its fair share of oinkers. Slobs. Chum-bucket bottom-feeder low-lifes who would do anything to make a buck. To dirty cops who weren't any different than the scumbags.

This pig must be someone's pet—or who knew what else nowadays. Like porking. Maybe it had been the pig's hooves on the bathroom window? The porker had come trick-or-treating, calling for old Rennis to open up. But, when old Rennis didn't answer, the horny pig came in after him, yelling his name because it was pissed.

A pig who could walk up walls?

Anything was possible tonight of all nights. Hell, Sinner knew if he stayed out long enough, he would come across all kinds of unusual creatures. Tarantulas. Snakes. And other things that belonged in the jungle—not the city.

But, Sinner wasn't looking for animals in this concrete jungle. Nor did he care whether animals had souls or not. No, why bother with things lower than man.

So, he didn't, walking down the street in hopes of coming across another person. For people screw the pooch—or the pig—and all other sorts of animals. Beastiality it's called. And that same twisted thinking messes up the world for everybody.

If you can't beat 'em, join 'em.

And Sinner had, all-in. All-in that pig if he could find it. And if someone happened to wander in on it, the act and Sinner's appearance would have that person thinking

Sinner's mind had been twisting for a while to be so twisted. Little would they know, the first twist had started another lifetime ago, as Rennis, and had been twisting ever since.

Until tonight, when his mind could not torque anymore.

Maybe that's what had happened in the kitchenette? His mind, a braided pretzel, ran out of dough to shape.

But this weaving wasn't being performed by the hands of a baker. A baker would see there was no more dough to shape because the pretzel had been completed.

No, human hands cannot weave the mind without destroying it right away. All bending and warping of the mind are not physical. It is of a consciousness. A mindset. Everything that makes a human a human.

Therefore, the manipulator never runs out of dough to mold. Torque-pressure. Torque-pressure. This continues unnoticeable and gradual until one or more of the braids snap and come undone.

A convenient explanation—losing one's mind. Especially in a world where pleading insanity is one of the sanest acts. But, in Rennis' case, it would explain little. There was an element of truth to it, but truer still, something or someone, not of this world, yet in it, had transformed Rennis' core—inside-out. Sinner, inside Rennis, conquered him there, then manifested that conquering outwardly for all to see.

After Sinner had gone about a quarter of a mile down the street, no one was around. No life sounds he had heard so clearly from his three-roomed apartment. The same after half-a-mile.

Sinner wanted to be seen.

Where the hell is everybody? This is a city! On trick-or-treat night. Impossible.

Never had he witnessed this kind of desolation in the city. Any time, any place, even the seediest areas, there were always people out-and-about. And if not the locals, it would be the visitors, living it up before they headed back to wherever the hell they came from.

After wandering around for maybe a half-an-hour or

so—it was hard to tell because a watch didn't make the cut in his new wardrobe—Sinner finally saw a silhouette of another human being standing in an alley. An alley he recognized. One in which he had never ventured. For that alley was a home of sorts to a number of homeless people.

If you call two brick walls not connected in any way a home. Hell, the alley counted as outdoors and Sinner doubted anyone referred to it as indoors. He wouldn't.

For that reason, during the fall season, many of the homeless started seeking more complete housing, so they had something over their head to keep rain, sleet, and snow out of their hair and four walls to retain warmth.

If they could find such a place. Not all of them would. Especially when it had to be free. A few might; most wouldn't. They all knew the odds weren't in their favor. Shelters were few and usually only took so many.

So, almost all of them would return to the alley and take their chances against Mother Nature. If she was kind, they might make it through the winter. If not—

Yet, every spring, the alley would be full again. Replenished with homeless people who found some comfort being in the presence of others in the same predicament.

Except for the lone silhouette in the alley, where were they now? At this rate, who knew when Sinner would see another human being? Such a thought signaled in his mind but originated from someplace else. An urgency followed that this opportunity must not be missed. So, rather than chance not running into another person, Sinner entered the alley.

To say old Rennis had decided to enter the alley would only be partially right. Less than a conscious choice and more of a mutual agreement between him and his new identity, Sinner, would be more accurate. For they had entered the alley together as one, but Sinner was at the controls—attracted to the silhouette like a carnivore to meat.

As Sinner proceeded toward the silhouette, an uncontrollable, glutenous desire for the flesh of the first non-family member participant to play a vital role in *who* he was to become—*what* he was to become—growled his stomach in hunger pains.

As animalistic it might sound, it wasn't far off. Selfish to the utmost, yet intelligent enough to reason. All too human, such characteristics—yet not.

What had entered the equation through Sinner trying to figure out *where* everyone could have disappeared to? *How* could a city this populated all of a sudden lose its populace? *When* did it happen? *Why*? And, ultimately, *who* or *what* was responsible?

And *goddamnit*, why had he been left behind? Along with this asshole in the alley. Why had they been spared? Maybe, the asswipe in bummer alley had some answers.

But Sinner's *him*, his true nature that had hidden itself all of those years under his *self* had never surfaced to be known, forbidden to be seen behind a skin veil, a lie tucked away under his wife's and kids' noses—like a booger high up in the nostril.

Where his *self* had never amounted to anything, perhaps his *him* could have made him someone to be reckoned with in this shitty world. *Self* never was nor will be essential. Nor had it ever distinguished anyone from others. Quite the opposite. *Self* is sexless, straddling the line on damn near everything, and therefore unable to stand for anything. Lines distinguish. And riding it makes a person indistinguishable. A *trans*, as in transgender. Transatlantic, as in both sides of the Atlantic ocean. Or transgression, when crossing the mid-line.

Him, on the other hand, stepped him off of that good-for-nothing line. Maybe only a step, but enough to know he was a man. Whose name, Sinner, moved him farther from that non-specific line called *Self* by distinguishing him from women and a vast majority of other men. Even if they had shared the same name, it still reduced the group he would be categorized in.

Assumptions had that transformability to make the assumer look like an ass. But still, they needed to be made. So at the risk of being an ass, Sinner assumed there must be a shared similarity between him and the unmoving silhouette in the alley. Bummersville alley, where bums alleyed.

October's wind stirred the air. A mix of piss, shit, vomit, and other scents, he had no interest in, attacked his nostrils and watered his eyes as if he had been punched in the nose.

Which he had. Those types of scents had co-cocked him before. Recently, too. In that unfit apartment building, Mr. Russel had let go to hell in a handbasket.

October's wind was, essentially, empty, too, but still able to blow those odors too heavy to dissipate into Sinner's face, a fog, which could only be pushed.

As Sinner walked deeper into the alley, the more he felt like a *what* than a *who*. It was as if he had lost his humanity. More detached than when he had first looked into the alleyway a few moments ago. Answers to all of those questions he had about what had happened meant less now, dissipating as he walked toward the silhouette. The only soul he had seen since his wife and children back at the apartment. Who stood about center alley, under the lone light attached to the right brick wall.

Nor did Sinner care any longer about any similarities they might have. In fact, whatever happened when he got to him, there shouldn't be enough time to find out. Being *special* meant exclusivity. Space was limited for one—*him*—Sinner.

There was that word again—*him*. Life had become all about *him*. And even if he was transforming into a *what*, he didn't want to hop back on that line again by being an unspecified *something*. Not now. Not after he felt like he had taken a turn for the better back at the apartment by going from a *nobody* in this world to *someone* to be reckoned with. How it would all materialize, he didn't know, but he felt elevated, somehow superior. Superior to his family. Superior to this loser in the alley. Superior to everyone.

Ghostly, Sinner approached the silhouette from behind, not wanting to be noticed. Exactly what he was going to do when he got there, he wasn't sure, only this approach seemed best.

Sneaking up from behind wasn't the most domineering move, but could be, especially when it was smart to do so. Besides, this felt right. Was working out right. Because, although the whole thing seemed strange to Sinner, it wasn't any stranger than how this had all started in the apartment.

Equally strange, not once did the silhouette move, just standing there with its back to Sinner the entire time. Maybe, watching the other end of the alley for any number of reasons.

Whatever they were, Sinner could care less, never giving it another thought. All he cared about was achieving the element of surprise. Not only for the person but also for Sinner, because he had no clue what exactly he was going to do.

The closer Sinner came, it became apparent the silhouette was real, not a mannequin or something bizarre like that. Its stillness had him wondering just that, but it had been confirmed. For the person had farted. Not that Sinner could smell it in *this* alley, but he had heard it. Flatulence, no question. Nothing exotic about its delivery. As straight forward as they come.

It had to be a man. Few women broke wind like that, except when alone, which this person may believe they were, but it didn't sound like a woman's fart. His wife had ripped a few during their marriage—never prior while dating—and not once could any of them be mistaken for a man's.

No, closer now, the silhouette was a man—a large man, tall with girth. Not fat by any stretch of the imagination, for his shoulders were wider than his waist. Regular haircut, not long or buzzed. Dressed normally, too, in blue jeans, sneakers, and overcoat, maybe a shirt collar barely sticking up just inside the coat's collar, but it was hard to tell.

No matter. It was definitely a man. The light about center

alley wouldn't lie or play tricks on him. Nor would his eyes. Neither would dare, even on Halloween, where tricks nowadays were seldom played, because the holiday had become all about the treats.

Man or woman, this would go down the same. And what was going to go down became more apparent to Sinner, matching the drive that drove him out of the apartment. But, knowing it was a man adrenalized him more.

So, Sinner hurried now, impatient to bring about another anticipatory high. Afraid to come down from the loft he looked down from. And what he saw from up there was everybody else, trying to dethrone the king on the hill.

With a blonde-haired pop-singer mask clothes-pinned to the front of his wife's dirty undies, work boots on his feet, an old orange t-shirt with a disfigured pumpkin face on the front, and his boy's red and black mask around his neck watching his back, Sinner ran toward the man.

And, don't forget about that butter-knife butchered face of his, which grew uglier as it clotted and hardened. Not much skin remained on his face. What did, amounted to nothing more than receded, tightened concaves, especially where his lips used to be. With his teeth exposed to the gums, his head resembled a skull covered in a thin layer of flesh with a mop of hair on top. Few things this Halloween would out-scare the sight of Sinner, who reached behind his own back as he ran and pulled the butter knife out from between his ass cheeks and his wife's underwear.

He wasn't surprised it was still there. With pinching ass cheeks forming a tight crack and his wife's underwear snug on him, together they had formed a near-perfect sheath.

But he had achieved the element of surprise. This fucker wouldn't know what hit him.

Knowing this didn't make any difference to Sinner, except for he was more obliged to carry-out the act if that's what *him* inside wanted.

Which it was. That's all this force had wanted this Halloween. Not tricks, or treats, or make-believe scares.

Halloween had turned into those things, which was far from its genuinely frightening beginnings, where ghosts and spirits would return to Earth and people tried many ways to hide from them as not to be recognized or did things to try to keep them away.

But Sinner would not be tricked so easily. Somehow he knew all of man's methods as if he had witnessed them all before he was ever born. Before the festival Samhain. Before Halloween was known as Halloween. And well before the calendar had been invented to say it was October 31st.

Each year on the same anniversary—October 31st—ghosts and spirits have returned among the living. For all human species were created with a spirit. Ever since the first Neanderthal death, they have returned for a time, then went back. Abel died by Cain's hand and was the first to return. Then, all who had perished in the great flood. Exponentially, through all Neanderthal deaths and their variants up through homo sapiens, the dead, who find their way, return.

How Sinner knew all of this, he didn't know. History wasn't anything that had interested him, nor did he have the acumen for it. Names, dates, specifics would be quickly forgotten or mashed up in his memory.

Still, despite how he had felt about it, he knew it; it interested him now—to a point. This newfound killing gig was more his speed. The speed of *him* inside old Rennis, whose name is Sinner, way before Sinner had taken old Ren as his own back at the apartment.

The entity named Sinner inside the man who used to be named Rennis had willed the flesh and blood by using Rennis' will to kill his family. Every day, Rennis had seen himself in his children. And what he saw was a royal loser who could never catch a break. So, when he had killed them, most of his hurt and frustration had been taken out on their still-developing faces more than any other part of their bodies.

Not seeing himself in his wife's face, Sinner had left it alone when he had killed her. Sure, there were times he hated her, the same way anyone might at times toward another, but never more than he had hated himself. And no one in this world hated *him* more than he did.

But, never in a million years would his wife ever let him kill himself, let alone the children. For as bad as it was at times, they were life-partners, through mostly bad and sickness with very little good and health. Therefore, it only stood to reason he had to kill her first—so he could trick the children.

Why Sinner—old Rennis—had thought of this stuff now, at this moment, with a butter knife in his hand raised to kill a man in bummer alley was beyond him. Way beyond, from a place where flesh and blood can't go. Call it heaven, hell, or the afterlife the living can't go there until they die and only the dead can come back on Halloween.

Suicide had entered old Rennis' mind more than he had liked. If the powers that be, a deity, the universe, fate, destiny, life, or another human being had reached out to help him turn his life around for the better, the initial thought of taking his own life would probably never had happened, let alone linger.

But no one gave a damn, so exiting thoughts lingered. They tend to, when—other than his wife—not one person out of billions on the planet, or deities, forces, or otherworldy life could care less whether he lived or died. And the older he got, the more he thought about it, multiple times a day.

Which had escalated today to not only involve himself but others, by taking as many as he could with him before leaving this unfair world. A reflection of Sinner's will which had transferred to old Rennis upon the foreign entity entering him in the kitchenette. From then on, anyone stupid enough to try their luck against this weirdo wearing women's underwear would have their hands full.

Or cut off, no matter how big the dude was. Every hard-on eventually goes limp, so will this non-aware target. And as old Rennis, now Sinner, swung the butter knife down toward the shoulder-neck area of this poor bozo, making this *jism-prism-easy* by standing with his back toward him so long, the inadequacy of the weapon entered his mind.

But, he had the element of surprise on his side. Yeah, this guy, homeless or not—probably not—would be Rennis' first non-family or familiar kill since his family back at the apartment.

Not true for Sinner, who had mastered crossing realms and had done so for sixty years since had he had figured out how. And every cross into the land of flesh and blood had resulted in Sinner crucifying quite a few materials.

When the butter knife descended in a sweeping arc toward the crevice of the man's neck and shoulder, the man turned around, reversing his view. Blood covered the entire front of his body, including his face, which was *cut-up* like Sinner's, but differently and beyond flawless repair. Whatever he had used must have been sharper than a butter-knife, because, although deep crevices of pink flesh covered his face, their edges weren't frayed, for the skin had been pared from the flesh.

Including the lips, which had been removed as Sinner's, leaving only skeletal teeth for a mouth.

The butter knife missed the head, neck, and shoulder area entirely. With the man facing him, it ended up leaving a slice through the front of the guy's coat. From what Sinner could tell, only the coat had been damaged, not the shirt or flesh, but there was so much blood on the front of it, it was hard to tell. Even the rain hadn't rinsed it off.

Simultaneously, something sharp entered Sinner's lower abdomen. Whatever it was went in easy. Caught off-guard, Sinner had lost all momentum; the butter-knife fell out of his hand to the wet macadam. Dingy teeth separated on his face, but without lips, he couldn't express the shock. Nor could his striped face, which stung, as his burned fingertips had earlier only worse, from stretching skin and flesh that had already begun to mend.

Only the widening whites of Sinner's eyes expressed

anything, seeing a skinned skeleton staring at him and noticing the flesh around its eyes twitching with effort from turning the knife handle around completely, which spun the blade inside Sinner, stirring his guts.

When the blade flattened with the ground, the man dropped to a knee, turning himself sideways as he did, and pushed on the knife with both hands, as a Samurai might with a sword. A shred of orange flapped like a flag in the wind—the orange Halloween t-shirt with the peculiar pumpkin face painted on it.

Sinner's ribboned face and grinning teeth looked down. He saw what had penetrated him—now that it had been pulled out of his body. A large hunting knife, covered with blood and strands of his inner workings, had left a gaping fissure along the right side of his abdomen and out his side.

When Sinner bent forward slightly for a better look, insanely interested, the two cliffs of flesh met like plate tectonics. Strands of intestine dangled out between them like pink snakes burrowing out of rusted dirt. Then, as he straightened, the cliffs of flesh separated; a maroon waterfall fell over the bottom.

All Sinner had now was his fists, so he swung his right one down toward his stabber. The gash in his side widened and the fowl alley air entered it as blood flowed out.

Letting go of the knife, the man reached a hand up and grabbed Sinner's wrist on the downward swing and squeezed with a power Sinner never could, even using both hands.

Sinner's wrist collapsed under the pressure. Just about every bone snapped or detached, limping the wrist and rendering it useless.

A punishing blow landed center gash the hunting knife had created. Looking down, Sinner saw a big fist with the hunting knife sticking out its side.

The pain there worsened and the horror nearly popped both of Sinner's eyeballs out of their sockets when they watched the fist and knife enter the cleft in his abdomen and disappear inside. Excruciating pain and the loss of blood thickened the fog to near blackout.

It appeared fake to Sinner. Like bad deception art that had failed miserably.

But it was really happening. The guy's massive hand and the knife were inside Sinner, for he felt the bulge of them, like a monstrous, murderous tumor.

A loud scream echoed in the alley—Sinner's—followed by a loud suction sound when the man pulled his hand out of Sinner and the knife sliced through more of his flesh on the way out. The last few remaining bones in Sinner's wrist snapped when the man used Sinner for leverage.

Mister Big let go of Sinner's un-operable wrist and opened and closed his hand to stretch it after being under tremendous pressure. Through the fog, Sinner saw that the man's fingertips weren't burned, as he had done in the cooking grease, but had been skinned—probably with that humungous hunting knife.

Even when it came to killing, there were others better than Sinner. Always someone better.

In the rain, Sinner fell to his knees in the alley; both men now near eye-to-eye. Near, because Sinner had to look up at the formable killer. Who wiped one side of the blade of the hunting knife across Sinner's hair, then the other side before sheathing it at the hip.

They stared at each other—two men with *cut-up* faces and skeletal teeth. Despite their similarities, they couldn't be any different. For the man stared at his victim, hellbent on taking as many with him as he could. Same as Sinner, one might say, but Sinner's count would never match. Sinner looked upon his killer with awe.

It seemed no one had made it out for trick-or-treating tonight. What had happened and where everyone had disappeared to, Sinner didn't know or care. Maybe this guy had killed the entire city for all he knew? Including his own family before venturing out for all of the others?

Impossible, Sinner knew, so there must be others. Somehow, someway, more like Sinner and this guy. Guys and gals who had grown tired of the world. Tired of losing. Tired of living. Who had murdered their families, erased their identities by scratching out their faces, their fingerprints, and went out for trick-or-treating to get themselves some more.

Hell, this guy had done Sinner a favor. It didn't matter how, by who, or by what, Sinner was checking out tonight, one way or another. It'll just be a little sooner than he had expected.

The big man had got him. So what? Sooner was better than later. He would just be leaving this world without taking as many with him as he had thought.

Hoped was a more honest word. Rennis had never taken a human life before today. In taking his family's, it made him feel powerful. Invincible. A rush he had never felt before. Better than sex. More potent than any high. Yes, *hoped* because he wanted to feel all of that again. Things he hadn't felt to that degree during this shithole of a life.

Truth be told, Sinner wouldn't have stopped until either someone had stopped him or when he had reached the point of exhaustion where there was only enough strength left to end himself.

Why couldn't Sinner have met the big guy later that evening? After Sinner had his fill. That way, he wouldn't need to leave any strength for himself. Kill two birds with one stone, essentially: Sinner could kill one more and the man in the alley could have finished him off. Perfect, really. Couldn't have been planned better if he had tried.

Or, maybe it wasn't Sinner's place to take anyone's life. Outside of his family's, that is. He could only assume killing them was meant to be, for no one had stopped it. Or, stopped him, for that matter.

But he had been stopped in the alley by the brute. Convincingly. Who reached both hands inside Sinner's stomach and began to fondle his insides. Easily, the most hair-raising, pore-opening experience in old Rennis' life to-date, feeling large hands exploring his inner cavity. The occasional finger-poke of the stomach or just them occupying space, pushing intestines together birthed sensations he never knew existed.

But Sinner knew.

Then, the ultimate feeling ... *of what?* ... conflicted him. *Degradation? Awe? Violation? Inferiority?*

Exactly. Sinner didn't know how to sum up all of the different emotions simultaneously hemorrhaging and flooding him. It was one of those unexplainable, indescribable things that ultimately goes undescribed and unexplained when no one can accomplish either. Which usually indicated just how unusual the circumstance. At that moment, he felt, as much as he could imagine, like the first man, maybe Adam, assigned with the task of naming the newfound feelings he had felt.

But he wasn't the first man. Others had felt this sensation before him. Those who had served in war or fell victim to body-opening tragedies. Which had not been many, when considering how many humans have lived on Earth.

For this large man before him was doing the unthinkable and must be of higher intelligence to even think of it. Sinner knew he would never have thought such a thing—this nightmare happening to him. For he felt his killer's hands around his intestines, stroking them across their length as if wiping the outside of a long hose.

What the hell this guy was doing was beyond Sinner. It all was. Why everything tonight had happened.

But the night wasn't through. Nor was the man, who wiped the outside of Sinner's intestines with his bare hands. Big or small ones, Sinner couldn't tell.

It didn't matter. Now, Sinner felt the hands moving vigorously inside his stomach. Why, he had no idea. Based on how it felt, it was as if the man might be rubbing them together, wringing his hands inside Sinner's abdomen as if washing them in the sink.

Then, the man pulled his hands out of Sinner, who could feel the void. The large hands were coated entirely in blood, which looked more like maroon-colored, plastic gloves than bare hands. For there wasn't a spot of skin visible anywhere. Not from what Sinner could tell.

Without hesitation, the man placed his hands over his own face—his *cut-up* face—and began smearing Sinner's blood all over it.

Before Sinner knew, he felt the big guy's hands back inside his abdomen, moving around, then back out.

This time, the man rubbed Sinner's blood all through his hair, scrubbing at times, as if washing in the shower.

As if it was meant to be, it began to rain harder, pelting the top of both men's heads. Sinner's killer rinsed off his hair and face as if rinsing off shampoo and soap.

When he had finished, the rain slowed. This man, *being*, must have an entity inside him worthy of the rain's obedience. Someone of importance from time's past who knew to enter someone with physical attributes which would allow him to go the distance.

Sinner, himself, had crossed over many times. Too many times. Because with each cross, spiritual senses and awareness begin to deteriorate. Faster for some spirits than others, depending on the spirit. When Sinner had seen the butter knife in the kitchenette, he had mistaken it for a butcher knife. How unfortunate for Sinner—but worse for old Rennis, whose body suffered for it.

A light rain fell, the alley glistening wet. The lone light shined down like a spotlight on the man, who stood over Sinner, looking down at him. No doubt, this dude had the size and skill to wipe out many. It would take at least a handful of guys with superior skill, some badass weapon or chemical, or a mob to stop this guy. Maybe that's why a city this goddamn big was as empty as it was. There were guys like him and even more ruthless spread all across the city—state—the world. Human lives being snuffed out by guys like the one in front of him. The fact that blood only covered his front and not his back said a lot. This guy keeps everything in front of him. And, as Sinner knew well, he was hard to sneak up on.

Fine. Less work for Sinner. As much as he had wanted to do more killing, old Ren's vessel was bleeding out.

Rennis emerged from within himself and felt his life slipping away. The fog so thick, it distorted his vision. Rest seemed easier than doing all of that senseless murdering.

The massive human placed both of his bloodied hands around Rennis' neck. He lifted him off the ground into the air, high enough to be staring at what remained of the pumpkin-face his kids had painted on the orange t-shirt last Halloween.

As the man looked up at his victim, Rennis' feet dangled off the ground. Barely cognizant, Rennis wondered why he had looked so long. *Was he remembering my face? Why remember? How many did he have stored in those memory banks?*

"I know that's you in there, Sinner," the man said.

"Who?" was all Rennis could muster.

The man's eyes narrowed with an intensity Rennis nor Sinner had ever seen in any eyes before. They saw right through Rennis' eyeballs into where most don't see. The man saw Sinner, the spirit who had crossed into the land of the living many times on Halloween, camouflaged in a different form, Rennis' body, but it did not fool him.

A guttural sound, a grunt, rose out of the man and then he answered, "Cain," followed by, "Join me."

While light rain fell, reflecting through the alley light, the powerful man held Rennis off the ground by the neck. Steam gathered at the front of Rennis' body and was absorbed by the big guy.

Immediately, Rennis' body went limp, so the man dropped him. Face-first, Rennis landed on the wet macadam. It smelled like piss.

Sinner wasn't inside him anymore.

Out of the corner of his eye, Rennis watched the man turn around and walk away, toward the other end of the alley, not threatened by his victim on the ground, nor should be, knowing death would handle the rest from here.

Fitting, really. Rennis didn't want to think about Sinner or his killer moving on to someone else. Jealousy, he knew, not in a relational way—in a killer way.

Low-life living had to end in low-life dying. Despite how Rennis had felt earlier, he had never moved up. But, he was moving *out*—of his body—just as Sinner had vacated him a moment ago—just as Rennis had abandoned his family and apartment.

He wondered if anyone had found them yet? Unlikely, because there didn't appear to be anyone around *to* find them.

Then, a disturbing thought entered his mind. He had killed a woman and two children, but not another man. Not like the alley brute had so skillfully taken him out—a failure right up to the end.

Rennis' eyes opened and closed frequently. Death was close.

When his killer had reached the end of the alley, someone had surprised the big guy by hitting him over the head with something large enough that took two hands. The big man stumbled.

That was the last thing Rennis saw. His final thought was, "I wonder if it was a rock?"

SURVIVE

A lunatic is running after me.

There I go judging again. Why did this woman have to be a looney? Maybe she was one of the hundreds of thousands sick in the city and needed help.

No. I don't believe that. What would make her think *I* could help her? Nothing. I'm not a doctor. If she needs help, why didn't she go to one of those testing tents or a hospital?

Because—she doesn't need help. I'm the one who needs help. I'm out of shape and she's gaining on me. No doubt, to harm me. Possibly kill me.

It all started when she had seen me across the street. I was on one side and her on the other. Not that I had noticed her right away. My mind scrambled about one thing in particular. Something I had come out for and couldn't find.

When I looked across the street to see if there were any stores that might carry what I needed, that was when I saw her staring at me.

Without question, she was staring at *me*. I know, because we were the only people on this strip.

Now, when a younger woman stops and stares at an older man like me, an attractive woman from what I could tell, her eyes alone can witchcraft the shit out of a seldom-used wizard's wand—if you catch the spell I'm casting.

My wand stiffened so hard a hint of uncomfortableness resulted. And, yes, it had been awhile. Under normal circumstances, the world could stress-press life out of folks easier than squashing a grape with two fingers.

But, these weren't ordinary times. Far from. No, these were extraordinary times. Not unprecedented, but had happened only a few times in the history of man's existence. Only a few things have impacted the entire world at once as this has. Not a continent or country had been spared. And the rising death toll—

She had run toward me.

For whatever reason, the woman had started sprinting right for me. And, ever since, she had been gaining on me. Even with a two-lane street lead on her, she had been gaining ground. My snake, transformed into an unbendable wand, didn't help. Nor did my hesitant start from the shock of what was happening.

Fear had jumpstarted me into motion. No lie, as cowardly as this might sound, I ran like my life depended on it.

Run like a rabid dog was chasing you people used to tell me when I was a kid. *Or anything that you're scared of and you'll run faster.*

Pretending might make you run faster than you usually would, but never meant it would be fast enough. Too many factors went into it. Stamina being one. There was no doubt in my mind that the woman chasing me had more favorable factors than I. And what I lacked, fear—not pretending, for I didn't have to pretend—fueled to delay the inevitable. At some point soon, she would overtake me. To do what, I could only guess. And all of my guesses assumed the worst.

Her footsteps slapped the pavement right behind me. Faint, but I heard them. My heavy breathing drowned them out.

"Stop!" she said with a hint of exhaustion.

It sounded right into my ears as if she were standing directly behind me. So close, there was no need to yell.

Believe me, lady. I want to stop.

"Accept it," the woman said. "Accept the end."

Of me, I assumed. How she would do it, I had an idea, but it was difficult to fathom. A gun, maybe? A knife? With her bare hands? All unlikely, but still possible.

No question, I knew how. I couldn't believe it, but it was the most probable.

Christ, I can't go much farther.

Something wet splatted against the back of my neck—bird poop, perhaps. I have short hair—always did.

Not at that angle.

"My venom," she said. "Get high on it."

Fuck! The bitch had spit on me.

Her hand brushed my back. Another brush, then a grab of my shirt.

"Stay away!" I yelled as I arched my back and tried picking up speed. "Leave me alone!"

"Death never quits."

It was true, Death never does.

My shirt stretched, then, finally, she lost her grip.

No matter my effort, it wasn't enough to put any distance between me and that crazed broad behind me. Maybe running was a mistake. Perhaps I should have kept my strength and faced her from the start.

Jesus, I had to stop.

"Join us," the woman said, "before it gets worse."

Worse? Than this? I'm dying here.

I was too exhausted to say I wasn't interested. But, she was right. With what was happening in the world, the experts seemed to agree with her.

I slowed down and she ran into my back, tugging at my shirt and trying to get a better handle on my arms to seize me.

This was it. My life came down to the next few moments. Either I would make it out of this alive, or—

A gunshot sounded behind me.

A second, then a third. The last one, I felt wetness spray against the back of my head and neck.

The front of the woman's body pressed against my backside. I felt her breasts squish against my shoulder blades; then, her body slither down mine.

Panicked, I started to run again and kicked her head with my heel.

"Freeze," a man said in an unwavering voice. "Police."

Tripped by the woman's head, I fell forward on the sidewalk. Then, I froze—a toppled-over statue, lying on the walkway.

"Stay down," the officer commanded.

Complying was easy, as tired as I was. Hell, I didn't even bother trying to see what I could. So exhausted, in fact, I couldn't hold my position and toppled over onto my back.

An officer bent down, looking at me through the glass of a SWAT helmet. "Are you alright, sir? Were you hit?"

His voice was different. "Hit?" I asked in confusion.

"Yes, sir. Were you shot?"

"I, *uh*…"

"Just check him," the first officer ordered.

The young policeman placed a hand behind my neck and helped me into a sitting position in time to see the other officer, wearing SWAT gear, pointing his pistol down at my chaser and poke her body with the toe of his boot.

"What's going on?" I asked the officer beside me.

"Hell on earth," he replied all too quickly.

"Donner," the other officer said. "That'll be enough."

"Yes, Sargent."

The Sargent lowered his gun and, surveying the area, made his way over to us.

"Sir, I'm Sargent Volka and this is Officer Donner. We're here to help."

"You already did," I said and meant.

"You okay to sit up on your own?" Donner asked.

"I think so."

"Was he hit?" Volka asked Donner.

"He's got blood on him," Donner said, "but I don't think so."

"Sir," Volka said to me, "do you think you can stand?"

I nodded I could.

Officer Donner helped me to my feet. We rose together, then he said, "Sargent."

It didn't sound right to me. Something was wrong. Maybe I had been shot.

Donner removed his hands off me and showed his right glove to Sargent Volka. It was torn. Blood was on his exposed skin.

Volka turned away, then said reassuringly, "It'll be alright, Donner. Just don't touch him, your face, or anything."

Donner didn't look so sure.

Right or wrong, it came out. "She spit on me," I offered.

Volka locked on to me. "Where?"

"My neck."

"Oh, God," Donner reacted.

"Donner!" Volka shouted, then said in a lower voice, "You're alright."

"What do I do, Sarge?"

"Tuck your hand in your armpit and don't move it until I say."

"What about getting back?"

A determined look of the Sargent's eyes into ours made us believers in him.

"Let's move out," Volka said and, with his pistol at the ready, he led the way.

Tired from running, I hoped wherever we were going wasn't far.

It was. Farther than I had wanted to go. But at least I had protection and company.

Blocks away from where I had been attacked, it finally occurred to me that the officers had left the dead woman there having never called it in.

When we arrived at the precinct, the place was in utter chaos. People crowded the building, trying to get in. All law and order seemed to be deteriorating by the second, soon becoming a thing of the past.

Sargent Volka boomed his voice for everyone to step aside, but it was as if they didn't hear him. With all of the commotion, maybe they hadn't.

Then, Officer Donner removed his hand from his armpit and raised it out in front of him.

"My Sargent said to move, God damn it!" he yelled.

People ignored the young officer. Until Donner screamed, "I'm infected."

Heads closest to Donner turned and saw his hand. Sweat from his armpit had nearly cleaned all of the blood off, rendering it pink, but there was still enough there along with the tear to get their attention.

Layer by layer, more heads looked back at the young officer. Gradually, the commotion tapered to silence.

Volka's eyes narrowed, watching Donner. With pride, I gathered, but it was hard to tell.

"That's better," Donner said. "Now, unless you don't want infected, I suggested you make an opening."

Donner's hand may as well have been Moses' staff because they all parted like the Red Sea as Donner led the way with his hand stretched out before him. I followed and Sargent Volka brought up the rear.

As we neared the door, Volka passed me.

"Joe," he said to Donner. "You can't."

Donner stopped.

Volka grabbed my shoulder with a gloved hand and pulled me toward the precinct door. Passing Donner, he said, "I'm sorry, Joe. I really am."

As I passed, I could see the shock on Donner's face, but also understanding. I told him, "Thank you."

At the door, Sargent Volka let go of my shoulder, told me to wait here, and entered the precinct.

My face must have looked as shocked as Donner's because an older gentleman standing next to me expressed pleasure in my shunning.

I waited. What else could I do?

It wasn't long before Sargent Volka returned and made an announcement.

"Officer Donner," Volka started. "Raise your hand so everyone can see you."

In seeing it, the crowd cowered, remembering Donner's words.

"Anyone needing or wanting to be tested," Volka continued, "follow Officer Donner to the back of the building." He nodded at Donner that he had this, that he was still serving this community, then continued, "He'll lead you to a testing tent where healthcare professionals can help you. But you must cooperate. Form a line behind him, remaining six feet apart from each other at all times. You must remain in that order. Any problems and you'll find yourself being escorted away from here. Everyone will be tested and seen, so please wait your turn."

Surprisingly, everyone followed Sargent Volka's instructions. It must have been what they had wanted all along. Now they had it; they were civil again. Law and order had been restored.

Donner led us through an alley to the back of the precinct. As people rounded the corner and saw the tent, clapping started.

Officer Donner, myself, and four others entered the tent

first to be tested. When it was over, we waited.

And waited. Nurses warned to stay at least six feet away from one another.

Night came and still no results. People were hungry, including me. Bellyaching got no one anywhere, except warnings from the law, namely Volka.

Restless and afraid, people were tired of keeping quiet and to themselves. Trying to strike up a conversation with someone four to six feet away had re-ignited the chaotic commotion from earlier. People moved closer to one another to hear or be heard.

As much as the nurses had chaperoned us to keep our distance, most people ignored them. It took Officer Donner radioing Sargent Volka to come out and keep the peace. One appearance by Volka calmed things down.

Dinnertime had come and gone. So had the hours. Amazing how when hunger pangs subsided, you weren't hungry anymore, but that what's happened. Everyone seemed reserved to the fact that knowing their test results were more important than eating.

Nurses appeared out of the tent. Only a handful of people were allowed to leave. Pockets of murmurings spread throughout those of us still waiting, until Officer Donner threatened them again with his hand raised.

"You might not even be infected," a man yelled back.

Others nodded and expressed their agreement.

So, Donner, quick of mind, slid his radio out of his belt and threatened to call Sargent Volka. The back of the precinct turned quiet once more.

Finally, at almost 10 p.m., Donner was called back into the tent. It could be because he was an officer of the law or to find out his test results.

I would have bet on the latter, but as names were being called not in the order we were tested, I started to worry.

By the time the seventh or eighth person had been called, a definitive pattern had emerged. So far, most had been called back into the tent, while a few had been summoned to the alley.

Others waiting also seemed to notice, our eyes meeting in unspoken agreement. Who knew for sure exactly what each of us was thinking, but I, for one, assumed that the tent was good news and the alley wasn't.

Not seeing Sargent Volka for a while, people carried on long-distance conversations, monitoring their distance, as did the nurses from the tent.

After a while, Officer Donner had joined them. From the tent opening, Donner located me and gave me a thumbs up. I assumed that meant he tested negative.

Someone from inside the tent yelled, "Hallelujah," and I knew my assumptions had been correct. Not long after, an "Aw, fuck me!" from the alley removed any remaining doubt.

Although I went in second after Donner, I was maybe the twelfth or so person to be called—into the tent.

A deadly virus had shut-down every country on every continent in only a few months. Schools closed for the rest of the year. Colleges for the rest of the semester. Businesses closed their doors until further notice. Sports already into their seasons canceled what remained, while those gearing up for the start of theirs quit before getting starting.

A Hollywood disaster script happening in real life. Store shelves were empty. Curfews set. People told to stay at home. Cops and military personnel strolled the streets.

How many times in life does everything cease?

Not ever. Not in my lifetime, anyway.

Once the nurse cleared me, Officer Donner approached, expressed his congratulations, and said that Sargent Volka had radioed him and we were to meet him inside the precinct.

Inside was equally chaotic, just less crowded. Thank God, more than half were police officers, busy doing their jobs. That was the only way this could be allowed, especially with Volka present, who met us in the hallway.

Everything going on didn't seem to bother the Sargent, who winked at his partner the kind that expressed he was glad he hadn't been affected.

"We're waiting on a room," he said.

When he got to me, let's just say, it lacked relief.

Not that he wanted me to be infected or anybody else. Nor did he seem like the type of guy who wanted to deal with this shit all because a virus had hopped-skipped-and-jumped continents on the backs of traveling people.

Like outside, we waited and waited.

Finally, at a quarter 'til eleven, the door opened and two officers and a boy about twelve came out. Perturbed, Volka ignored them and led the way inside.

The room stunk. God knows how many people have been in here today, let alone the last few months. We sat in scuffed wooden chairs around a metal table. Right off the bat, Volka asked me to listen and save my questions and comments until the end.

Donner must have known what was coming because he slid down in his chair to get comfortable.

Volka spewed out information. How hate groups all over the world were hellbent on attracting the virus and using it as a weapon against humanity to bring our kind to extinction, so we would stop ruining the planet. Some of their more subtle tactics involved touching and spitting on food, coughing and sneezing in faces, and *fingerfucking*—Volka had used specifically—whoever and whatever their little whore fingers could reach. They had many slogans, but one of their more common ones was *Leave it to the animals.*

Now wasn't the time to debate whether we were animals or not, so whatever Volka divulged, I listened.

More importantly, apparently, I had survived a murder attempt. That's right. That woman had the virus, belonged to a local cult of human executioners, and had tried to infect me in hopes of killing me.

Jesus! All I could think about were zombie movies.

But the more Volka shared, the more I realized these

weren't re-animated walking dead-heads interested in eating brains. In many ways, this was much worse. These were living, breathing, thinking, domesticated persons sacrificing the rest of their lives by willingly contracting a fast-spreading lethal virus so they could infect others before they died themselves, in hopes of wiping-out humanity.

Good, Lord! If he was either, I couldn't say.

Then came the crux. After all of this time, Sargent Volka asked me my name.

"Ray," I answered.

"Ray, Raymond, or something else? It's late."

"Raymond."

"Raymond what?" the Sargent asked as he wrote my first name on the top of a form.

"Christmas."

Volka dropped his pen, looked at Donner, then at me. "*Christmas.* Are you shitting me?"

"No."

"Let me see your license."

I pulled out my wallet and slapped my driver's license on the table. The hour and events of the day were unwinding our civility.

Without picking it up, Volka leaned over and read my information. Straightening, he said, "Christmas it is, then."

While he jotted down the information off of my license onto the form, he asked me questions.

"Mr. Christmas, why were you roaming the streets when you know you shouldn't have been?"

It was true. I did know. Mandated first by the Governor of New York, then by the President himself.

"My wife needed medicine," I answered.

"Your wife needed medicine," Volka essentially repeated. "Do you have it on you?"

"No."

"No?"

"They were all out."

"What does she need?"

"Protonix. She has a hiatal hernia and acid reflux."

"She has indigestion?"

"No, it's more serious than that."

"Why were you not wearing any protective gear?" Volka asked.

"My wife and I don't have any," I answered.

"You could have followed recommendations. Made a mask. Wore some type of gloves, even winter ones. Couldn't you? Or your wife?"

"I guess so."

"You guess so? You should know so."

"What do you want me to say? You're right."

"Not all of the time, but usually."

I raised my eyebrows and pursed my lips. I felt like an idiot—which I was.

"I'm issuing you a warning," Volka said.

"A warning?" I couldn't believe it.

"Yes, a warning. I can do better than that if a warning isn't to your liking."

"Take the warning," Donner said.

"Alright, fine," I whined. "I've been warned."

"Officer Donner," the Sargent said. "I don't think Mr. Christmas is taking the warning to heart, do you?"

Shaking his head, Donner said, "Sorry, Mr. Christmas, but I have to agree with Sarge. You're not taking the warning seriously."

"I am," I replied. "You guys may have saved my life. I'll never forget it or what you said."

"Make sure to tell your wife what happened," Volka said.

"I will. She's probably worried sick." I snapped my fingers. "A call. I get a phone call, right?"

"You're not in custody, Mr. Christmas. But we'll do better than a phone call. We'll drive you home."

My wife opened the door of our apartment, saw me, cast a spell on me with some choice words, then hugged me, crying. Seeing Sargent Volka and Officer Donner standing behind me in the hall, she pushed me aside and cursed them up and down Broadway until she had written her own show. To their credit, they took it like men who had experienced this before: Volka probably from the wife and Donner most likely from his mother.

When I finally got a word in to tell my wife that they had saved my ass, she hugged Volka then Donner, then scolded them that one of them should have called to let her know I was okay.

"You're right, Mrs. Christmas," the Sargent began and went on to apologize.

"You've done this before," I said to Volka.

"More than I can count," he said.

"I take it you're done."

A purse of the lips and nod told me he was.

I grabbed my wife's shoulders and turned her so we faced one another.

"Roxy, they didn't have your…," I started.

"Here it is, Mr. Christmas," Volka interrupted.

I looked down and saw he was holding a prescription bottle.

"You had asked us to keep it for safekeeping," Donner added.

"Yes," I said, taking the bottle. "I forgot."

Reading the label, it was a thirty-day supply of Protonix 40mg. No name on the label, but who cares. When I handed it to my wife, she kissed both of my cheeks.

Volka and Donner blushed as if she had kissed *them*.

She should have.

An apartment building is not ideal living quarters while under a stay-at-home quarantine. It's been two weeks since New York had buckled down enforcement of this order and tenants continue to ignore it. If they're blowing-off quarantine, it's safe to assume they're not worried about spreading the virus.

My wife and I have been cooped up in the apartment,

other than when she gets the mail out of the box at the bottom of the steps every Tuesday and Friday, and I left for the first time yesterday in search of her medicine.

We're due for some more groceries, but the last two deliveries barely amounted to anything. If it's not on the shelf or in storage, we're not getting it. Based on what the news has been airing, the shelves are bare and I'm guessing so is the storeroom.

Same with my wife's medicine. Three times we tried ordering and each time they were canceled.

Sure, demand for nearly everything was higher than supply, but come on. I kind of understand food, disinfecting wipes, gloves, and masks, but come on—a shortage of Protonix? Aren't the companies making more of this stuff, so people have what they need?

It sure doesn't seem like it. A lot of it stemmed from scared people, stocking up. Then there were those trying to help, such as hospitals, scrambling to order what they need now and what they'll need later. I'm okay with it as long as no one is hoarding the stuff. Hell, if I were smart enough, I would have done the same thing, especially my wife's medication.

What I'm not okay with is price-gouging. Those assholes who placed gigantic orders before anyone thought of restricting how much people could buy only to sell the shit online at rape-me prices should face infection of the virus. I mean, a hundred bucks plus shipping and handling for one container of disinfecting wipes that usually costs less than ten bucks? That's raping someone.

Christ, the building seems to get noisier every day. Constantly, doors open and close in banging fashion. Loud conversations echo in the hall. Arguments, where you hear every goddamn word, float up from the floors below ours and sink from those above. Honestly, some days, I don't know which is worse: going into work or staying here and listening to this shit.

The only noise my wife and I don't seem to mind comes

from children. Wheels scraping the hall floor as they ride. The bounce of a ball or two. Running. Pretending. Laughing.

Our children are grown and out-of-state. Before this started—the virus—we called them every second or third week. When the virus hit, we called them every day to make sure they were okay. Now, we called them twice last week and once so far this week. It's not that the situation is any better. If anything, it has gotten worse. Every day, confirmed cases and deaths keep rising. We're calling our kids less because they are calling us more.

My wife and I call our parents more often, too. Both of my wife's parents are still living. In Texas, so we don't get to see them that often. Definitely, not now with travel bans enforced.

And I call my mom more. Sometimes twice a day. She's older than my wife's parents by a good ten years. I was a *Holy Shit!—How did that happen?—Did you forget to take your pill? accident baby*, my dad used to say. Explaining what it meant botched it worse. *Kid, your birth falls somewhere between a whackjob accident and a condom breaking accident.*

Like that meant anything to a five-year-old. I never knew why he felt like he had to try to explain it, but occasionally he did. One of those years in my early-forties—I can't remember which—it finally made sense. I laughed my ass off.

He's been gone for five years already. I still can't believe it. Oh, how time flies.

My parents never wanted kids. So, my mom used to say to my dad, *You should have gotten a vasectomy.* Then, he would say, *And you should have tied your tubes.*

The conversation went on-and-on.

You tricked me into bed. I wanted to wait until I was married.

Tricked? Oh, no. You make it sound like I offered you a piece of candy.

You were sweet.

I was, wasn't I. I was just glad you weren't sour. Remember the

182

penny test?

Then they would kiss and go off somewhere where I wasn't. Thank God I didn't witness more. Funny how the mare visited me those nights—nightmares.

For two adults who never wanted kids, they turned out to be pretty good parents. Outside of them mentioning they didn't want children at the start, I never felt unwanted.

Five years. Damn, time flies.

I just got off the phone with my mom. So far, she's living better than most. She lives in one of those come-and-go-as-you-please retirement homes here in New York. At least that was the policy before the virus hit. They have been on lockdown for some time now. Maybe one of the earliest to cut-off from the world. Apparently, it worked because mom said no one living or working there had tested positive for the virus.

Mom thinks one of the best things the home had decided was allowing workers to live in the buildings, so they weren't leaving and returning with the virus. Not everyone could, so they were furloughed until this crisis ended. Any slack was picked up by volunteer residents, who welcomed the responsibility.

When my mother moved into the apartment, she vowed she would never cook another meal again after doing it for so long. Well, it didn't last long. Every holiday she comes over and helps my wife in the kitchen. Now, she is putting those culinary skills to work at the home by working in the kitchen no more than four hours per week. Honestly, she sounded great over the phone. It must be doing her good.

That's why I say she's doing better than most. I mean, where else could you find seasoned cooks, cleaners, caregivers, and all other domestic skills than in a retirement home—men and women who had tackled indoor and outdoor chores for years in most cases.

People forget how diverse the state of New York is. Believe it or not, there are grassy sections within and around the city that needed mowing and trees and hedges to trim.

My mom was in a great place. All of her needs were met and whatever else she might need, the home would assume the effort in trying to get it. Also, if anything should happen with her physically, the staff was right there to help.

Still, I worry about her. The damn virus attacks indiscriminately, but preliminary data suggests it preys on the elderly and those who suffer from other health problems.

Sounds cowardly to me. But a virus isn't a coward or anything; it's only a virus.

That just so happens to prey on living things. And replicates. And spreads. Between all living things. Across oceans to every continent. And no matter where you live: city, town, village, or otherwise—dense or sparse, high or low, land or water—right down to the paved street, dirt road, or walking path—it can find you. Without looking for you. On that delivered package. Groceries. The mail. In the air you breathe. And you don't know it's there because you can't see it or smell it. No indication or warning you might be in danger. Something so small can grow into a huge problem and truncate your life. A deadly game of hide-and-seek played at the highest stakes. And we're the hiders, confined to our dwellings, trying to survive—as is the virus. On one hand, the ideal killer, the worst of all enemies. On the other, an unintelligent thing, because although it needs you to survive, it turns around and kills the very thing it needs to prolong its existence.

From our bed, I heard my wife unscrew the medicine bottle—Protonix 40mg—in the bathroom. The one Sargent Volka had handed me to give to her. Yes, a month had passed. A fart lingered longer.

Numerous times, she had tried contacting her insurance and doctor but was yet to hear from either. Her current prescription was for thirty days. I remember her trying to increase it to ninety, but our insurance is the bastard child of what insurance was supposed to be and kept it at thirty.

As far as her doctor, well, apparently, someone had carried the virus into the office and it spread like wildfire through anyone who stepped foot in there, including her doctor.

Rumor has it: in examining patients exhibiting flu-like systems, he had a terrible habit of—not wearing gloves or washing his hands.

Can you believe that shit? A doctor?

After hearing that, I didn't feel so stupid in not being prepared myself for this attack on humanity.

Roxy shut the bathroom light off and laid beside me in bed.

A loud gasping and bouncing of the bed startled me out of sleep. Seeing my wife sitting up in bed, coughing, I trotted to the bathroom and returned with her water glass. Every night, she brought water up with her to take her pill.

She must have been lying a particular way, not as propped up as she should have been, where stomach acid had flowed through her esophagus and tickled her throat.

Burned, actually. Acid burns and eats away. And she had choked on it.

Stomach acid should not be anywhere else but in the stomach. Thus its name. A critical valve where the esophagus meets the stomach should allow food and drink into the stomach and block acid and such from coming back up. That is if it was operating correctly.

My wife's doesn't. A hiatal hernia there makes it not close properly. So, she takes a pill that helps to calm the acid and repair any damage it causes.

Roxy took a few sips of water, trying to soothe her burning throat. How she would deal with this was a process, it really was. She'll wait for things to clear and settle before sipping more water and repeat until her throat feels a little better. That would be the best she could do and expect for the next couple of hours. It will take at least that long for the burning to subside before she felt normal again.

As I said, it's a process.

It's been a while since she has had an episode. It burns me she has to have them at all.

When Roxy leaned back against her propped pillows, the hesitancy was easy to see. I would be the same way. Who knew if it would happen again.

Thankfully, it had happened twice in one night only once. Her sitting up for the rest of the night usually curbed it from happening again. Genuine rest wouldn't happen either, but I think my wife thought it was worth it.

While she leaned back against her pillows and closed her eyes, I went to the bathroom and took a leak. Washing my hands, I saw myself in the mirror and mentally complained about looking like an albino prune.

Curious, I opened the medicine cabinet and checked her pill bottle. When I saw there were only two pills left, I figured she had skipped taking one tonight.

I felt responsible.

And, like a failure. Unable to provide for my wife in these precarious times—when a good husband would have.

This was unacceptable. *I* was unacceptable. So was our insurance and her doctor. I wanted to do something. Had to.

I went to her side of the bed and asked her if she was alright. She nodded she was, so I kissed her on the forehead, rounded the bed and laid down.

Then, it hit me.

Fifteen minutes had passed since the idea had hit me. I wished it had hit me harder and earlier than now. I would have had more time to think it over.

No, on second thought, I'm glad it happened this way. If I had longer to think about it, I'm not sure I would go through with it.

That was to say, I'm sure. Dead sure. If that's what it took, then I hope my wife would forgive me and know I was only trying to get her what she needed.

Maybe I would fail as before. But at least this time, *my* skin would be on the line, along with my wife's already there.

What I was about to do was about as selfish as anyone could be. Cruel, too.

Damn. Now, every conceivable word of what this was came to mind. From *aggravated assault* in the As to *theft* in the Ts. Not to mention, Sargent Volka had issued me a warning.

To hell with it. My wife needed the medicine, didn't she? If she ever choked on her own acid or vomit because she didn't have the pills and something worse happened than an episode, I'd—I'd—

That could never happen. Not as long as I'm around. So, I need to stop thinking and get on with it.

Restless, I got out of bed and checked her water. It was nearly empty.

"I'm...*alright*," Roxy scratched out.

"You will be," I said a little too forthright. "I'll get you some fresh water."

"I'm goo...," she started before a coughing fit exploded.

"No, you're not. I'll be back."

A trip to the kitchen during the night was one I had made many times. Hell, I'm sure I have probably sleepwalked there on a few of them. I poured out the old water in the sink and went to the fridge for some fresh. The damn dispenser on this fridge made a lot of fucking noise when operated. Besides, water tended to splash onto the floor. It ended up being more of a hassle in having to wipe it up than just using the spigot.

My wife has the same issues with it but still finds it worth it for the filter. That, I had to agree with. In being lazy, I've tasted our spigot water and every time ended up dumping it back into the sink.

Instead of using the ice machine gadget, I opened the freezer, grabbed a few cubes with my hand, and dropped them into the glass. It was a hell of a lot quieter.

Before heading back, I thought I'd see what was loose in

the fridge to nibble on. The only thing easy was a bowl of black olives. Not my first choice. Or my fiftieth, or hundredth. I popped a few into my mouth anyway.

Standing there, eating them, I left the door open for the light and scanned the counter for something more my speed. The toaster oven. A block of knives. Hand-washed dishes on a drying mat. Back to the knives.

I studied them for too long. Not knowing their names but knowing which blades went into each slot. We've had that block for years, maybe as long as we have been married, so I knew it well.

One last look at the knife block—while eating an olive— then I returned the bowl to the fridge, closed the door, and headed back to the bedroom.

"Here, darling," I said, handing her the glass. "I should have been faster."

She drank half of it and let it settle. A few minutes later, the glass was empty. Like I explained before, it was a process.

Without asking, I went to the kitchen and got her some more water. And a few more olives I didn't need. It was an excuse to use the light—to look upon the knives sheathed in the wooden block on the counter once more.

At some point, I must have placed the glass inside the fridge, because there I stood, watching the knife-set as if it were a movie, eating olives like popcorn, and holding the bowl.

When I came out of it, I looked down at the dish and only three olives were left.

No use in putting the bowl back in, so I polished off the last three and set the bowl in the sink.

My fascination with the knives scared me. I thought I knew me, but maybe I didn't know myself as well as I had thought. To what extent I was willing to go for my wife lengthened the more I thought about it. *Great* lengths, apparently. How great hadn't been entirely defined, but—

No—wait—now it had.

Not a particular distance. Not in a certain time. No, this was vaguely specific. *All the way* meant what it meant. However far. However long it takes to get there. To do whatever needed done to accomplish the mission.

Finally, my wife fell asleep. Not that it took longer than usual after an episode. Recovering from an acid burn in the throat would naturally take time for anyone to feel comfortable enough to trust falling asleep. I was just glad she was able to get some shuteye.

At two-thirty in the morning, the whole idea of putting off my plan until tomorrow night started sounding good to me. With my wife settled and my body in that sometimes hard to find comfortable lay, postponing seemed the way to go.

Besides, I'm not sure I'm an *all the way* type of guy. Not in *this* sense, anyway. Sure, I've gone all the way with my wife plenty of times, but when it came to actual work effort in trying to accomplish a goal, well, I'm more apt to *meet you half way*.

But my mind wasn't settled. Far from. The damn thing kept seeing those two pills in the bottle.

Sure, two was enough to postpone—one for tomorrow night, the second the next night.

Then, that would be it.

To say it didn't haunt me would be a lie.

It had to be this morning before light.

So, I laid there another fifteen minutes, planning, before getting up, dressed, and out the door by three.

The hallway reeked of contamination. I didn't plan for this virus very well. No, failed on that one. Not that it was my first failure after all of these years, nor would it be my last. My wife and I didn't have any masks, gloves—

Wait a minute! What was it Sargent Volka had said at the station?

Why didn't I think of that before? My wife has a pair of rubber gloves under the kitchen sink she uses when she cleans.

Ugh! This air.

I went back inside the apartment and, quietly, got the gloves from under the sink.

Now, something for the air.

Seeing the hand-towel, I tried wrapping it around my face like a bandana, but it was too short.

Okay, now what? Something longer. One of my wife's scarves?—No—A wool scarf from the coat closet.

As I wrapped it around my head, so it covered my nose and mouth, I didn't know if it would stop the virus or not. Doubtful, but maybe it would deflect it or something. Have to be a perfect shot to navigate through into my orifices.

If anything, it would help to block the smell. A small thing, but it was something.

Damn! That took too much time.

Forgetting about covering my eyes, I left the apartment wearing my wife's bright yellow rubber gloves, which covered my hands and forearms up to the elbow, and a predominately-brown plaid scarf around the lower half of my head.

I must look like a dufus, but at this hour and what I was about to do, who cares.

The four-block walk from my apartment building to this one didn't take long. Speed-walk more like it. Fast enough to work up a lather. The rubber gloves and wool scarf had heated things up a bit.

So had my fear. Walking the streets at night in this city, or any city, wasn't my bag. In fact, going out, in general, was against my nature. I was a homebody, no question. The Governor didn't have to tell me twice to stay-at-home. Hell, outside of going to work and minor errands, I was already on lockdown and practicing social-distancing before the orders came down.

Still, the blasted virus messed up our lives. Being out here, as an example. Exposed to all of the usual dangers along with the threat of a highly contagious virus that attached to things and lasted there for days, can be transmitted from person-to-person by coughing, sneezing, or breathing within six feet of one another, and can hover airborne for hours. One virus, a triple threat. Six feet was about right—under the ground. At least it wasn't airborne-airborne.

Inside the lobby of the apartment building, I pulled down the scarf for some air. At first, it felt good. Then, a similar stench as in my building infiltrated my nostrils and the scarf went back up.

Okay, now—what floor did that guy say he lived on?

Like an ass, I tried to remember when I didn't have to. The mailboxes would tell me.

Ah, there's his name. Apartment 19.

Shit.

Unlike my building where a number-letter system was used—number for the floor and letter for the apartment: mine was 6F, sixth floor, apartment F—apartment 19 here didn't tell me anything.

It'll be light soon.

Calm down. Now, what floor did that guy say? Seventh? Eighth? Ninth, maybe?

Something like that. A low number. Single digits below ten.

Man. I don't have time to knock on apartment 19 on each floor.

After trying to think of another way, nothing came to mind. I had to knock anyway, so what was a couple more doors?

Who would answer the door at this hour?

Bad vibes. The rattling kind. Enough to make me consider throwing in the towel—or scarf—and chalking it up as another failure.

Can't. Failure wasn't an option.

I could say I'm with—I snapped my fingers while I thought—someone to do with this virus. C.D.C. W.H.O.

Local police.

That was it. I'll say I'm Sargent Volka with the New York City Police Department. We're checking on residents because … because … think dammit … because a tenant is believed to be hiding a dangerous fugitive in their apartment, so we're checking all apartments and making sure residents are okay.

Maybe it would work. It would have to.

Unless—he recognized my voice.

I'll try disguising it. I'm not sure I'll be good at it, but I'll try sounding as authoritative as Sargent Volka had sounded.

I took the elevator up to the seventh floor and located apartment 19.

While standing there, it occurred to me that I might get inside and only find a few pills in the bottle.

Jesus! Why didn't I think of that earlier? About as dumb as dumb gets.

Fuck it! Any pills I could get my rubber-gloved fingers on will relieve my wife's symptoms and buy me some time.

'Buy me some time.' Listen to me! I sound like a hoodlum.

I guess I was. If I wasn't one officially, there was a pretty good chance I might be one soon enough, depending on how this went down. Because, while getting my wife more water in the kitchen, I decided that, if it came down to it, I would kill Julius for those pills.

I knocked on the door of apartment 19.

A usual knock. Neighborly knock. Lacking authority. Not how Sargent Volka would knock in an intense crisis.

So this time, instead of using a knuckle, I banged on the door with the heel of my fist.

"Open up! Police!" I yelled.

I panicked. What if a neighbor comes out instead and sees me dressed like this, saying I'm the police?

"Who?" sounded from behind the door.

It might be Julius—I wasn't sure.

"Sargent Volka from the New York City Police

192

Department," I tried to say confidently.

A click sounded from the door being unlocked, then a rattle of the chain link unclasping.

When the door opened, a man stood before me—but it wasn't Julius.

"Hey," the man said. "I thought you said you were a cop?"

"I am," I said. "I was working undercover when this broke."

"When *what* broke?"

Bad vibrations again. The jarring kind. Impersonating a cop, no wonder I felt rattled. Seeing and hearing myself banging a tin cup across prison bars.

It had never occurred to me that if I got the wrong apartment and Julius didn't answer, I would still have to go through the whole rigmarole by checking the apartment and asking a few questions to keep up the appearance—and out of jail.

I didn't want to, but I did it. Finishing up, I risked asking the man if he knew where Julius Reed lived. To my surprise, he spilled, "Sure, I know Julius. He's on the ninth floor, apartment 19. Why?"

Without explaining, I simply thanked the man and went on my way.

I banged on the door of apartment 19 on the ninth floor.

This was turning out to be more work than I had anticipated. Irritated and tired, I banged on the door again and said, "Police! Open up!"

I didn't think anyone was going to answer.

"Who?"

I recognized Julius' voice from behind the door.

"Sargent Volka from the New York City Police Department," I said more confidently than last time.

"What's this about, officer?" Julius asked through the door.

Smart man, that Julius. Not so swift at work, but, in these

matters, he sounded competent enough.

"We're searching every apartment," I said. "Making sure tenants are okay because, well, I'll explain inside. We're trying not to alarm everyone at once, nor do we have the time to explain through everyone's door. Now open up!"

A few long seconds passed.

Then, I heard Julius unlocking the door and unclasping the chain link. The door opened, and there stood Julius.

"Raymond?" he said, looking confused.

I hesitated, staring at him, him at me.

"Why did you say…"

Before either one of us knew it, I had forced my way into the apartment and closed the door behind me.

"Has your mind been touched?" Julius blurted. "What is this? Why are you here?"

"I need something Julius," I said. "Actually, my wife needs something. If you give it to me, I'll walk out of here with nothing bad happening."

"*Nothing bad happening?* What are you talking about?"

"I need all of the Protonix pills you have. Now."

"My PPIs? That's what this is about? At four in the morning?"

"Now, Julius. Every single one."

He raised his chin and said, "Or what?"

The moment came faster than I had anticipated— because I hadn't anticipated anything.

His apartment was small and open—a single dwelling for a single man.

"Well?" Julius asked.

Does he have company?

Too late, now.

"You have 'til three to start talking, or I'm calling the cops," Julius said.

Instinctively, my eyes scanned the apartment. Tiny as it was, it didn't take long to see what I had hoped to see—

He pointed at me. "And why are you dressed like that?"

—a hanging set of knives attached to the kitchen wall.

I looked at Julius and a deeper part of me that had surfaced maybe only once or twice over the years said, "In case your blood splattered."

That part, I had thought out: the knives not what I had said. I knew there wouldn't be time to rummage through drawers to find a weapon.

"In case my blood splattered?" Julius questioned, his face shriveled like a giant prune.

"Sure," was all I could say. "Why the hell not."

"Did you just threaten to kill me over Protonix?"

"Forty milligrams."

"You've been cooped up too long. Why the hell didn't you just order some over-the-counter ones until you worked out Roxy's prescription?"

If I had only contacted him earlier, this whole mess could have been avoided. I couldn't come right out and say I didn't think of it, although it was true.

Boy, did I botch this up. On top of that, him remembering my wife's name weakened my resolve. Hell, I must have only mentioned her to him a few times.

Who knows? Maybe I talked about her more than I realized.

Avoiding the question, I said, "Come on, Julius. Just get the pills and I'll be on my way."

"Fine," he said. "But not all of them. I'll give you a few to hold Roxy over until you get this straightened out."

Julius turned and headed for the bathroom like it was a done deal.

I thought about grabbing a knife and making him give me all he had or else.

'Or else what?' he had asked, and now I ask myself.

Julius returned and went into the kitchen. When he came out, he handed me a clear sandwich bag with some pills in it.

I took it; the pills looked familiar.

Pointing at the bag, he said, "There are ten prescription

in there and a few non I keep as backup. Your wife should start doing the same. I didn't give you the bottle with my name and information on it, so there isn't any evidence of your intrusion. Now please leave."

What could I do or say, other than leave and say thank you.

One more thing, actually.

"You're not going to call the cops?" I asked.

"I should," he said. "For all of the trouble you caused. You do know you can get in serious trouble impersonating a police officer, don't you?"

"Yes," I said, hearing the rattle of the cup along prison cell bars. "I'm sorry, Julius. I'm not thinking straight with this damn virus and everything."

"Well," he drew out. "Keep cool, man. Cooler heads always prevail."

"I'll try. I really will."

"And take care of Roxy, huh. You're lucky to have her."

Christ, I never thought about him being alone.

Walking toward the door and waving the bag of pills, I said, "I'm glad nobody had to lose any blood over these."

"Shit," Julius blurted. "You're not infected, are you?"

"A little late to be asking, but no. You?"

"Not that I know of. I've never been tested."

"I have and passed."

As I stepped into the hallway, Julius said, "Oh, that must have been a relief. For both you and Roxy."

"It was," I said, feeling that relief. "Thanks again."

Julius nodded and I headed down the hall.

After a few steps, I turned around and said, "Hey, Julius, with everything going on, how about I give you a call and we could chat a bit."

"Okay," he agreed. "But give me a few days to blow this out of my system."

I nodded. "Will do. And sorry, again."

"Honestly, you can't say that enough times."

"Next time, over the phone."

"Next time," Julius said and closed the door.

I stood there long enough to hear him lock and chain it. Then, I headed home.

Four-forty in the morning, nine floors down and four blocks to a warm bed. If I'm quiet, Roxy will never know I had left. Unless she had woken and didn't feel or see me lying next to her. Maybe she had gotten up and used the toilet.

That would be bad. Worse would be if she had another episode and I wasn't there. I would never forgive myself. She usually doesn't have two on the same night, but watch it happen tonight of all nights.

The elevator dinged and the doors opened. Looking out the lobby windows, I was surprised to see how dark it was still. Bleak. Nighttime could be beautiful at times, but from this view, *out-there* seemed about as abysmal as a rainy day that had ruined special plans.

Maybe it did rain. A smokey screen blurred everything.

When I stepped outside, the ground wasn't wet and the city didn't appear as blurry. Had to be the windows. God knows the last time they were cleaned.

Which was scary under the circumstances. In all of the excitement upstairs, I had nearly forgotten all about the virus.

Four blocks now, that's it.

Jesus, what a night! One of those segments of life you would rather have skipped.

While walking, it had occurred to me that this little excursion would not be over when I got back. My wife was sure to ask where I had gotten the extra pills.

Forgot that, too—until now.

The truth would work. I could say that Julius gave them to me. Which *was* true. But at four in the morning? She would think Julius and I had something going.

No, she wouldn't. She knows how I feel about *alternative lifestyles*. More like Julius and I had arranged an early-morning sunrise with some broads.

She wouldn't believe that either.

Christ, I'm tired.

I'm not sure if I had ever mentioned Julius to her or not. If not, I could say he worked odd hours, but then she would know I was lying. Our company was one of the first to shut down when the spread of the virus had picked up pace and many in the city were becoming carriers.

Boy, I wish I remembered if I mentioned him to her before or not. Even if I did, there had to be more than one Julius in the city. Hell, I could even say any other name had given me the pills and she would never know.

Two blocks to go.

Aw, hell. Being out in this crap, I would have to shower before crawling back into bed. That was sure to wake Roxy.

Come to think of it, so what. I did just get back from picking up the pills.

Okay, this was coming together. Sure, this concoction consisted of a cup of truth and a tablespoon of lie, but for the pills, I could swallow it down.

Of course, I'll take credit for thinking of trying to get our hands on some over-the-counter pills. Something she never mentioned if she had thought of it.

Almost there.

Oh, shit. What's this?

Someone came out of the alley and is just standing there, facing me.

So what? It doesn't mean it has anything to do with me.

I peeked over my shoulder.

Someone was running toward me. Just as that crazy broad had.

When I turned around, the person ahead was running my direction.

God, I hope they're running toward one another and not for me.

Out of the corner of my eye, a flashing shadow moved near the street. By the time I had turned and looked, another person appeared from behind a parked car and grabbed me.

Almost simultaneously, I felt more hands on my back. Before I could do anything about it, the scarf tightened around the lower half of my face.

I tried fighting back; honestly, I did. Their strength could only be described as primitive. As much as I wanted to get away, they wanted me more.

In no time, the person from my front arrived and clobbered my face with something other than a fist.

The one behind me pulled the scarf so hard that it slid down my face and across my neck.

I've never had my air cut-off like that before. The thought of my wife's occasional acid reflux episodes came to mind. How it made it hard for her to breathe normally—as I couldn't now.

While I struggled for air, to my horror, others appeared out of the shadows into view. More out of the alley, from behind vehicles, and emerging out of the city's shadows.

How many, I couldn't accurately assess under my plight. Let's leave it at a lot. And I could only assume the same was happening behind me.

Straight out of the worst of nightmares, in shadow, the newcomers casually walked toward me, unhurried, taking their sweet time. The total opposite of those attacking me.

Euphoria fogged and distorted my sight. A slowing down, if you will, with an unexplainable and contrary expedition underlying it. The immediate frenzy of the attack seen through bogged-down vision, delayed.

Druggies, I thought. PCP or some other drug had wired them to damn near invincibility.

Until the one directly in front of me showed me what he had co-cocked me with. Of all things in this world—a Bible. Not a small one either. Nor softbound or new. No, this sucker's hardcover had been handle-worn over the years but had been built to last. For my attacker made sure I saw the title by placing it directly in front of my face, impossible for wide eyes to miss even within the fog.

The others had joined and circled around me. Two of my

attackers had yanked the yellow rubber gloves off me and tossed them aside. Then, they braced my arms behind my back and stomped on the tops of my feet, warning that they stay flat on the ground.

Slowly, the book of books lowered like a falling curtain, unveiling a hood filled with darkness. A voice spoke out of the abyss.

"Do you accept the end?"

The crazed broad who had chased me had said something about accepting the end.

Its youth frightened me. Much more than if it had sounded demonic. Demons wanting to afflict harm was old news. So were humans out to overpower other humans.

But this was childlike. No older than late teens, early twenties. Sure, there were plenty of reasons in this world to be pissed-off, but for someone so young to have anger woven into their speech was wrong.

"Answer!" the dark-one demanded, raising the Bible in the air.

The scarf relaxed around my throat.

My windpipe wouldn't open when I tried to speak.

The hooded one waited.

"No," I scratched out. If I couldn't fight back physically, perhaps verbally. Doing so scared me and didn't seem smart but—

"No prophet is accepted in his own country," the blackhole said. "Perhaps, if you knew who I was."

The one before me slid the Bible into the kangaroo pouch of his sweatshirt and grabbed the sides of his hood with bloodied hands.

Holy Christ! I didn't catch that before: blood-stained Caucasian hands.

Deliberately slow, they removed the hood, unveiling the person concealed within.

At least I thought it would. Instead, a mask of Jesus Christ stared back at me; the face of my assaulter still unseen.

"I am your savior," Jesus said.

"The real Jesus wouldn't be doing this," I struggled to say.

"*Oh,* I wouldn't? I don't remember endowing you with the ability to understand the mind or ways of God."

"You couldn't," I said stronger. "You're just a man. A boy, I figure."

"In part, this is true. My other part is the son of God. It is a great mystery. As mysterious as two people becoming one in marriage, yet it is. Are you married?"

"No."

Those young eyes looking at me through the mask were as dead and unexpressive as a shark's. Without any hint of effort, they remained that way, as Jesus grabbed my hand and separated a finger from it.

He brought it before my eyes as he had done with the Bible, ensuring I saw it. My wedding band still around it.

"Take us to her," Jesus said.

Pain left me only shaking my head that I wouldn't.

"Don't you want me to save her?" Jesus asked.

Again, I shook my head *no.*

"You're in pain," Jesus said, taking my un-whole hand. "It will end. Willingly fall on the rock or be crushed by it."

Then, he did something I thought I would never see by placing the opened wound where my finger used to be up to the cutout mouth in the mask and sucked on it.

It hurt like a motherfucker. From his germ-infested mouth, I swore I could feel the infection tingling. An itch that could not be reached or relieved by scratching.

Jesus sucked on the opening for a while. A guilty pleasure he didn't seem to mind doing in front of the others.

Then, adding to the horror, when I noticed the others, they seemed to derive pleasure from it, too.

Will no one help me?

No, none here had any interest in doing that.

When Jesus finished, his fleshy lips and the plastic around the mouth of the mask were covered with my blood.

In a state of euphoria himself, Jesus said, "Take me to her now."

"No!" I shouted as loud as I could, hoping to be heard, followed by a sputtered eruption of emotion. "Never!"

"Some unbelievers need persuading."

"Nothing you do to me will change my mind. Nothing."

A blackened tongue emerged through the opening in the mask and licked up my blood like a blood-thirsty leech.

Moans and groans of pleasure came from the aroused disciples, watching.

After a final slurp, Jesus said, "I'll wipe the dust off of my feet. Only I have conquered death. People think it was easy. What they fail to understand is death never quits."

The woman who had chased me earlier had said something like that.

"Since you were born, it has been pursuing you, chasing you toward itself."

Then, Jesus' face enlarged in front of me, moving close to mine. So close, redness around the eyes and flakiness of the skin around the mask explained everything. This young man carried the virus and, based on his appearance, had for a while. I had seen enough on the news to make that out.

The son of God kissed me with bloody lips. Which was surprising enough. Opening his mouth and tonguing me with that black leech raised the disgust to a sickening level, I nearly threw-up.

If I could have, I would. Because his tongue entered my mouth and grew like a hard-on inside a vagina. Its tip reached my uvula—then amazingly beyond.

Banged upside the face with a Bible was one thing. Being choked by a tongue—a man's no less and diseased--was entirely another. And more dangerous.

I couldn't breathe.

Everyone watching sounded like they enjoyed what they saw, whooping and hollering, encouraging their leader. A king of sorts, who thinks he is Jesus; his lunatic followers his disciples.

Where was everybody?

The city, I mean.

Did no one hear? Doesn't anyone care about anyone else anymore? Or had this pandemic pushed humanity further into solitude than we already were?

If I had heard or seen, I'm not sure I would come to the rescue either, but I would at least call the police.

Maybe someone had for all I knew.

Part of me knew. With ninety-eight percent of Americans observing stay-at-home orders, what reason would anybody have for being up at what had to be about five in the morning?

None. The city that never sleeps slept-in later now because of the virus.

After being choked by the scarf, losing blood where my ring-finger used to be, and being deepthroated by a guy who thought he was the Christ, the lack of oxygen and loss of blood started taking its toll on me.

But I had worse problems. If Jesus was infected with the virus, there was no question I was now, too.

All I could think about was *Roxy*, and *I'm going to die*.

This virus has a high mortality rate. Some had died quickly, while others, like Jesus here, might last a while, even seem like recovery whispered you're going to make it, then *boom*, you're body clamps down from being suffocated to death and you're snuffed out.

Just when I was on the verge of blacking out, Jesus removed his tongue, breathing heavily himself, and I heard a whoosh of air as it flowed again. I dry-heaved and gagged, but nothing came up. What a strange experience.

But that didn't match what was happening now. As I fought to stay awake and alive, this wannabe savior licked my face repeatedly.

The halitosis alone damn near killed me. It smelled like sickness. Unfortunately, I tasted it, too. Being choked had cut off any sense of taste and smell, but now both registered and nearly broke the bank.

God, Jesus, whoever, whatever, I wish you would strike down this asshole and his hemorrhoids. Find this murdering fag guilty of impersonating the son. And, just in case, forgive me for impersonating a cop.

Whether I died from this or not, either way, my life would never be the same. Survivors of this germ would suffer ongoing complications from having it.

If I survive this and overcome the disease to be with my wife again, it would be nothing short of a miracle. Which was what I needed now. Someone to see, hear, and call for help or any kind of answered prayer.

Jesus' face filled my view; his eyes may or may not have stared into mine—it was hard to tell. They were blank. Still. Lifeless.

Yet, they looked at me. I was sure they would be the last thing I would see.

In some ways, I wish Jesus' face would have been the last thing I saw, not this guy's.

With a bloody face and bloodstained hands, Jesus removed the Bible out of his sweatshirt, raised it in the air, and said to his following, "His spirit is high on my venom. A venom of judgment on him and humanity."

The insane woman had said the same.

"For I am both the son and the serpent. Good and evil dwelling together in the same garden."

Those around shouted *amen.*

"As my disciples, so your venom should be shared in this judgment and administered accordingly to my word."

A sermon this was. A prophet he had called himself.

Jesus lowered his Bible, turned, looked at me, and said, "Let it be so."

His followers closed-in on me.

I tried to free myself. To fend them off. But I was too weak and outnumbered.

In a coordinated attack, someone spit into my mouth, then tongued it, while others tore off my clothes and bit me wherever they happened to be. Not a part of my body was spared. I felt wet tongues enter my ears. Spit spray my eyes. Mouths take turns swallowing my penis. Tongues lick my ass.

They were infecting me. Injecting the virus into me. Murdering me.

I knew I would not survive this. For a little while, sure, but in the long-run, there wasn't a long run. Not for me. A short sprint at best.

I tried to make peace with it.

I couldn't.

Despite the ignored prayer, I tried making peace with the creator, whoever or whatever it might be—just in case.

I wouldn't.

A part of me refused.

True, this might be the fruition of what the Bible referred to as pestilence, but that didn't prove the validity of scripture, nor the existence of God.

No one could question the virus existed. It was a non-discriminate killer, much in the same way scripture describes God as not a respecter of persons. And a proven killer as supported in the scriptures. So are people and much of creation, too—including Earth. With the church consisting of people, the church wasn't innocent.

Perhaps, all of creation contained attributes of its creator. How could it not? After God's image, scripture says more or less. Right down to a virus.

When my wife got the news, she was devastated. Obviously, I wasn't coming home. Although no one expressed to her as much, there was a high probability I would never see our home again.

And that cut. Worse than the bite marks all over my body, which itched relentlessly. We had lived there for more than twenty-five years, nearly my entire adult life, and about half of my life. There were many things I would miss. The bed where I slept so comfortably and made love to my wife. My recliner and TV, which had provided unplanned naps and mindless programming, which gave my brain a rest. Books and movies that I had gotten lost in many an evening.

But no one more than my wife. We have been married for longer than half of my life. Not adult life—*my life*. She was my best and only close friend. And I wouldn't have changed that. I liked being with her, and I hope she did me.

All of the things we did together bum-rushed my mind. I loved and hated recalling them at the same time. Reminders of everything taken from me: my wife, our place, our belongings, things we used to do and the plans we had made, our future, my future, my life.

Last I knew, despite my best efforts in describing all I could remember, there weren't any solid leads to who had done this to me. Apparently, I wasn't the first, for Sargent Volka had warned me about these radical groups, nor would I be the last. That infected group of fanatics was going to get away with it.

My wife came to see me. She hated having to go out in the muck of a contagious world, but she braved it.

I knew how she would feel and couldn't blame her. To say venturing out in public was risky was like the Surgeon's General Warning on a pack of cigarettes, only more vague. It was risky. But, being resolute, she came to see me.

Through a window.

In testing positive for the virus, it was the only way. I had been quarantined inside a hotel being used as a hospital.

The government had to get creative that way. Hospitals were packed to the walls. Any and all floorspace could not be wasted. And they lacked the equipment they needed. It was a mess. A real-life *holy-shit-hell-storm* depicted in books and movies come to life.

Not only *my* life, I had to remember, but everyone. So far, there were over two million confirmed cases in the United States alone and more than a million deaths. Like I had said, a high fatality rate.

When refrigerated tractor-trailers were parked outside hospitals for the collection of dead bodies, a lot of people were suffering loss—as my wife will—while I'll *be* the loss, placed reverently inside the back of one of those trucks before into the earth's ground or my ashes scattered.

Whichever my wife chooses, it's fine with me.

And, who knows, maybe leave this earth.

My wife and I held church every Sunday in our living room via the television. We used to go to church for many years, then stopped. Maybe we had forsaken the brethren since, but our Sunday's seemed longer and, because of it, more enjoyable. We got a day of our week back and I wouldn't change that.

Through the window, my wife looked like an angel.

She was. One of the few things in this world that made me think maybe God did exist.

I greeted her with a written sign held against the window that read, "Hello, Roxy."

My wife lipped *Hello* and touched the sign.

I held up my other hand, palm flat against the glass.

At first, she stared at it, then placed her hand on the glass over mine—the one with the missing finger.

I flipped my pre-written sign over and she read it.

"I lost my ring."

She started crying and lipped, *I know. It's okay.*

I put that sign down and held up another I had already written.

"I love you! Always have. Always will."

Her beautiful lips moved that she loved me, too.

I flipped the sign over.

"You're the best thing that has ever happened to me. No regrets with you!"

Usually, I'm not a crying man. But this was—was—

Through teared vision, I saw her holding up a written piece of paper.

"Are you coming home soon?"

This was our communication. As close as I could ever get to my wife again.

I held my response against the glass. "No one told you?"

Her chest raised and lowered. I could see no one had.

"No. I'm sorry," my note read.

She needed a minute. So did I. I didn't want to be the one to tell her.

After a moment, she wrote angrily and placed it up to the window, "What happened?"

"You skipped pill. Went for more."

She titled her head, pursed her lips, and couldn't contain her emotion. Then, she wrote another note, slower this time, and placed it against the window.

It read, "Buying time. Ordered generic from grocery store. Received today."

ABOUT **THE AUTHOR**

W. G. TUTTLE is an American writer of riveting science fiction, thriller, and suspense novels and short stories. He is the author of the novels Try To Sleep, Those Who Long, October Midnight, and War For The Spheres. He has also written numerous short stories, including Scranton October 1894, Vacation's End, Where Did THEY Come From?, and Standard Issue Spirits.

He also writes screenplays and intelligent non-fiction about stocks, investing, and trading.

Born: January 27, 1972, Binghamton, New York

Full name: Walter George Tuttle, Jr.

Spouse: Shawn M. Tuttle (m.1997)

Children: 1 son & 1 daughter

Alma mater: The Pennsylvania State University

Influenced by: Frank Herbert, H. G. Wells, Ramsey Campbell (Carl Dreadstone), Arthur C. Clarke, Isaac Asimov, Stanislaw Lem, William Peter Blatty, Ira Levin, Robert Bloch, Ian Fleming, Alistair MacLean

wgtuttle.com